PAUL AND ETTA

PAUL AND ETTA

by

RICHARD PARKER

Illustrated by GAVIN ROW

THOMAS NELSON INC.
Nashville • Camden • New York

No character in this story is intended to represent any actual person; all the incidents of the story are entirely fictional in nature.

Text copyright © 1972, 1973 by Richard Parker.
Illustrations copyright © 1972, 1973 by Brockhampton Press Ltd.

First U.S. edition

Library of Congress Cataloging in Publication Data

Parker, Richard
  Paul and Etta.

  SUMMARY: Paul, an orphan, and Etta, an only child, have problems getting along when Etta's parents decide to adopt Paul.
  [1.   Orphans—Fiction.   2.   Family life—Fiction]
I.   Row, Gavin, illlus.   II.   Title.
PZ7.P234Pau3   [Fic]   72–13011
ISBN 0–8407–6282–8

Contents

PAUL AND ETTA

1 . Paul

Paul was brushing his teeth when he heard his name being shouted up the stairs. It was Rosine, the housemother, calling him. She spoke in a funny way because she came from some other country, Belgium or France or somewhere. She even made his name sound different.

"Powl! Powl!" she kept calling. "Someone please to tell me! Is that Powl up from his bed?"

Paul couldn't answer with his mouth frothing and the toothbrush wedged in his cheek, so he went to the head of the stairs and grinned down at her.

"Oh, you. Powl!" she cried impatiently. "You forget it is your turn to set the table."

Paul snatched the brush out of his mouth and answered indignantly through the froth, spluttering some of it down the stairs as he did so. "It's not my turn. It's the twins' today!"

"We did it yesterday!" shouted the twins from the bedroom.

"Well, you shouldn't have."

"Yes, we should have," they chanted.

"You shouldn't!"

"Rosine told us. We all moved up one. Will's Mum took

him back on Wednesday, so we all moved up one. It's your turn today!"

Paul was cross because there wasn't an answer to this. He flung his toothbrush at the basin, wiped his mouth on his shirt sleeve, and stamped downstairs.

"Temper! Temper!" said Jock, a ginger-headed boy of eleven who was combing water onto his hair to make it lie flat.

A Pakistani girl called Sadi, one of Paul's special friends, was already halfway down the stairs. She turned and said, "I'll give you a hand, Paul." Sadi had long dark hair and beautiful eyes that always looked a little sad.

"Oh, no, you won't!" snapped Paul rudely. "I don't need any help to set a couple of stupid tables."

Sadi's eyes looked a little more soulful than usual. She stopped and waited until Paul had almost reached her and then gave him a quick push so that he stumbled back and sat with a bump on the stairs. She had jumped the rest of the flight and disappeared out of the front door before he could give chase. Rosine put her head around the kitchen door.

"What is this?" she cried, although she knew perfectly well what had been going on. "So now you want a little rest, do you?"

Paul was about to snap at her when he realized how funny he must look. Instead he gave a grin and went through into the common room where the two tables were. Still smiling to himself, he set all the places backward, with the knives on the left and the forks on the right, the saucers on top of the cups, the bread on the teapot stand and the tea cozy on the breadboard. He was just in the middle of turning all the chairs around with their seats away from the table when the children started coming through for breakfast.

Some of them laughed, some of them called him names, some just sighed, and Jock, putting on his high-toned voice, said, "Now here's a funny stunt to start the weekend. What a witty fellow you are, Paul Aintree!"

Paul felt his good humor restored. He sat down on his chair and prepared to eat left-handed, but Rosine, bustling in with the breakfast, soon put everyone to rights and made them all sit up properly.

Sadi sat next to Paul as usual. "I hope I didn't hurt you much," she said to him.

"I ought to give your hair a tug," Paul said.

She leaned her head sideways as if inviting him to do so and he did in fact give it a bit of a pull, though more for the pleasure of touching its cool smoothness than to be revenged.

After breakfast they all had half an hour's work to do, washing dishes, helping with the house in one way or another. It didn't take long because there were so many of them—ten altogether, although you couldn't really count the twins, as they were only six and anyway spent more time making a mess in the bathroom or hiding under the beds and giggling than anything else.

Paul finished his job of sweeping out the boys' bedroom, and when he had put the brushes away he went to see what Rosine was so busy at in the kitchen. She was putting icing on a huge fruit cake.

"What's that for?" he asked. "Is that for today?"

"Certainly not. This is special. It is for Jock's fête."

Paul was puzzled. "What's Jock having a fête for?"

"Because it is his day tomorrow." Rosine saw by Paul's expression that she was still not making her meaning clear. "Oh, you English," she muttered. "I am having the wrong word again. The day he was born. What is it called?"

"His birthday!" said Paul. "It's Jock's birthday party tomorrow. Of course."

"Do you want to scrape out the icing?"

Paul took the bowl and cleaned it out with his finger. Then he went outside and stood on the path wondering what he would do.

From where he stood he could see the next house through

the trees, but the other six houses that formed the rest of the Magsted Children's Home were out of sight. In fact, the Home stood scattered through a large wood. Here and there were clearings, and in each of these clearings there were climbing frames or slides or swings. Many of the bigger trees had thick knotted ropes dangling. But the best part, or at least Paul thought it was the best part, was the tree-walk. This went all around the wood, going from tree to tree with rope ladders near each of the houses. When Paul had first climbed up to it he had been giddy and frightened, it had seemed so high. He remembered that very clearly. It was the week after his seventh birthday, when he had first been sent to this place after leaving that house in Maidstone where he'd been so miserable. He didn't think about that time. He dreamed about it sometimes, but you couldn't help what you dreamed.

He climbed up the rope ladder and then started to walk along the planking of the tree-walk. He just touched the handrail on either side lightly with his fingertips. Jock could run all the way around without once touching the rail, but then Jock was eleven. Paul wondered if he would be able to do that when he was eleven.

He felt a faint trembling in the planking under his feet. It meant someone else was on the tree-walk. Paul stopped and took a firm hold on the rail before he looked through the trees to see who it was. He soon recognized a girl called Evelyn from the next house, going along a little way in front of him. She was moving very cautiously, shuffling her feet inch by inch and gripping hard on both rails. Paul was surprised to see her up there at all.

Evelyn was twelve or thirteen years old, but she acted like a baby. She couldn't talk properly, and most of the kids called her Eelin because that was what she called her-self. She had to have her meat and food cut up for her at mealtimes so that she could shovel it in with a spoon. Paul walked on, gradually catching up on the slow, shuffling figure in front.

Below on the ground, one of the housemothers was en-couraging Evelyn in her efforts.

"There's a clever girl! That's right, keep hold of both sides!" When she saw Paul coming along behind, she waved her hand to tell him to keep back a little. But Evelyn had felt his footsteps through the plank and she suddenly began to panic.

"Tome's toming!" she cried out. "Tush toff."

"It's only Paul," said the housemother. "You like Paul. He's your friend. He wouldn't push you off."

But the girl had lost her nerve now and could only cling to one handrail, crying fearfully.

Paul looked down. "I didn't mean to frighten her," he said. "I was a bit surprised to see her up here, though."

"No, of course you didn't mean to. Do you think you could help her somehow? The longer she stays like that, the worse she'll be."

Paul nodded and made his way along until he was stand-ing near the terrified girl. "Look, Evelyn, it's me," he said, putting his hand on her arm. "I'll help you, shall I?"

Evelyn turned her tear-stained face toward him and gabbled something about being frightened.

"You hold my hand, eh, and I'll help you along," said Paul.

He wasn't ready for what happened next. Evelyn was so relieved at seeing who it was that she let go of the handrail and almost threw herself at Paul, clutching at his shoulders. Being about twice as heavy as he was, she almost pushed him off his balance. One of his feet slipped off the side of the plank, but he managed to grab desperately at the rail and hold on with one hand while the other was holding the girl.

"Phew!" exclaimed the housemother from below. "I thought I was going to have to catch the two of you. Well done, Paul. Do you think you can manage, or would you like me to come up?"

"I'll manage," said Paul.

He kept talking to Evelyn and looking at her, and gradually, as she calmed down, he persuaded her to hold on to his right hand with both of hers so that he had his left hand free for the rail. When she obeyed him he started to edge backward along the plank tugging her gently after him, talking all the while so that she would look at his face and not downward, which might make her giddy and frightened again.

They were only two or three yards from the tree with the ropeladder, but it seemed to take ages to reach it. Evelyn could not be persuaded to take proper steps; she would only edge her feet forward an inch or so at a time and if Paul pulled too hard she looked frightened and stopped altogether.

At last they did reach the top of the ladder. The housemother had already come halfway up so she could guide and support Evelyn's feet on the way down.

When they all three stood on the hard, safe ground again, Paul and the housemother both were exhausted. Paul's knees were twitching in a very odd way and he had to put one hand against the tree trunk. Evelyn, however, seemed quite undisturbed by her adventures. All she could think of was the fact that she had actually been up on the tree-walk.

"Eelin tid it! Eelin tid it!" she cried, clapping her hands. "Eelin to it dain!" she added, suddenly running to the rope ladder and starting to climb it.

"Oh, no, you don't, young lady," cried the housemother, grabbing her quickly before she got out of reach. "Once is quite enough for one day." Then, when she saw this was likely to produce a storm, she added quickly, "Tomorrow you can do it again. Tomorrow, eh? More tomorrow?"

Evelyn said something which the housemother didn't understand. "What did she say?" she asked Paul.

Paul said, "She wants me to come too. When she does it tomorrow."

"Would you mind?"

"No. I'll help out."

Paul heard his name being called and turned to see Sadi waving to him through the trees.

"What?"

"You said you were going swimming."

"I forgot," shouted Paul.

"Well, come on now. I'm just going."

Paul ran off to get his trunks on, and then joined Sadi in the pool.

2 . The Lonely Only

Two or three weeks before this, Etta Milford stood on the edge of the lawn talking to a foxglove.

"If you'd only stand up straight," she said, "I think we'd be just about the same height. Let's see, shall we?"

She edged forward until her toes were covered by the large bottom leaves. The long spike of flowers rubbed against her face. The top curved over just level with her eyebrows.

"Not quite," she said. "I'm still taller than you are because there's a bit more of me up to the top of my head. You'll just have to go on trying, won't you?"

Etta didn't expect the foxglove to answer her; she was used to talking to things that didn't answer. She had a black-and-white rabbit that twitched its nose and a tortoise that didn't take a blind bit of notice. She had to do the talking for them.

She wandered slowly around the garden trying to think of something to do. She looked at the swing, but there was a bird's mess on the seat, and it wasn't worth the trouble to get a cloth to wipe it. She went on, and when she got to the climbing frame she stopped.

"No," she said a moment later. "I've done everything I can think of, and anyway you make me too hot."

At the end of the garden, near the little gate that led out into the alley at the back, stood the small shed that contained her bicycle, along with the lawn mower and various garden tools. She thought of riding down to the sea and then along the front and perhaps stopping at the stand to get ice cream. She often did this, but today it didn't seem worth the trouble.

Her wanderings had brought her to the open French windows, so she walked through, switching the TV on as she passed the set, and threw herself on to the sofa. There was a cowboy film on.

"Well, at least it's better than a ball game," said Etta.

But it wasn't better. The film had just reached the shooting part, which Etta hated. And what's more, it was on much too loud. Etta put her thumb in her mouth because it was shooting, and then tried to put her fingers in her ears to cut out the noise. She found she could just manage. She curled herself up on the sofa and watched the screen with glazed eyes.

A few minutes later her mother came in. Etta saw her mouth moving but couldn't hear what she said because she still had her fingers in her ears. Mrs. Milford looked angry and she moved across the room in an angry way. She switched the set off. Etta took her fingers out of her ears and sat up.

"Whatever were you watching that for?" demanded Mrs. Milford. "You know you don't like it."

"I wasn't watching it," said Etta. "I was waiting for it to be something else."

"And now you have your thumb in your mouth! I do wish you'd make an effort. A big girl of nine. What do they say at school?"

"I don't suck it at school."

Mrs. Milford didn't stop to argue. She hurried off down

the passage to the kitchen and started to unpack the shopping she had just brought in. Etta trailed after her but stopped on the way to look at her front teeth in the mirror.

"They're not sticking out, yet," she said when she reached the kitchen.

"What aren't?"

"My front teeth."

"Then you're very lucky."

Mrs. Milford turned on the faucet of the kitchen sink, threw the vegetables in, and then started to attack them with the kitchen knife as if they were her deadly enemies. Etta leaned on the door and watched.

"Can't you find something to do?" Mrs. Milford asked over her shoulder.

"No," said Etta.

"I thought you enjoyed reading."

"I do."

"Well, then."

Etta didn't answer, and for a while her mother went on scraping and cutting in silence. Etta wandered away and went to stare out of the front window into the street. The two boys who lived in the house opposite were kicking a ball up and down the pavement. She knew it was no use going out; they wouldn't let her play.

The glass misted up with her breath and she was just going to wipe it off but instead she wrote with her finger:

> *Etta, Etta, Henrietta,*
> *Not too bad but could be better.*

It was a rhyme her father had made up for her to skip to. And there was a nicer one that went:

> *Henrietta Milford,*
> *Long, tall, and thin,*
> *Has green eyes*
> *And a pointed chin.*
> *She eats up her taters,*
> *She eats up her fish*
> *And counts out her prune stones*
> *All round the dish:*
> *One, two, three, four, five . . .*

and you went on counting until the rope caught in your foot.

Etta turned away from the window and went back to the kitchen. The vegetables were finished and in saucepans on the stove, and Mrs. Milford was beating a batter.

"Pigs in a blanket," she said.

Etta didn't say anything. She watched the swirling batter making patterns around the beater.

"Can I phone Sandra?" she said at last.

"If you like. Do you want her to come over?"

Etta shrugged her shoulders. She drifted off to the telephone, but a few minutes later she was back in the kitchen again.

"Well, any luck?" asked her mother.

"She's gone swimming with her brother," said Etta. "Whenever I want her to play with me she's always doing something with her brother."

"Never mind. Look, set the table for me, will you?"

Etta began to set the things out on the table in a listless manner. "I wish I had a brother," she said, and banged the pepper and salt down hard on the table. "I think you and Dad were mean having only one." She banged down the breadboard, and the loaf bounced off and rolled on the floor.

"You are in a black mood, aren't you?" said her mother.

"Everybody else at school has got at least one brother or sister."

"Well, not everybody," said Mrs. Milford, and she began to say the names of other children. But Etta was certainly not in a mood to listen to reason. She picked the loaf up off the floor and thumped it down on the board, muttering fiercely to herself as she did so. Sometimes she felt she was really two people—one person fed up and bored with being an only child with no one to play with, and the other person, the other half of her rather enjoying the game, pretending to be more fed up than she really was.

Mrs. Milford heard it all going on but didn't say anything for a while. She put the sausages in a neat row down the middle of the batter, then she opened the door of the oven and put the tray on the middle shelf. She looked thoughtfully at Etta who was gradually getting the table

laid after a fashion—a very noisy fashion.

"You know," said Mrs. Milford, "it's not our fault. We wanted to have two or three children."

"I know," said Etta. "You've told me. You wanted another baby but the doctor said you couldn't. You've told me lots of times."

"Well, then. Why are we still talking about it?"

"It doesn't make it any better for me," said Etta sulkily.

Mrs. Milford sighed. "No, I suppose not. But it's something we can't change, so you'll just have to get used to it. Anyway, there are compensations for being an only one."

"What are compensations?"

"Well, I mean, you have a lot more things than most children have. More toys and so on. And you have a room all to yourself. When I was your age, I never had any nice new clothes. I always had to wear the dresses my sister had grown out of. And when I had a new doll for my birthday, my brother broke it the very next day."

"On purpose?"

"No. He dropped it out of the bedroom window with a parachute, and the parachute didn't open." Mrs. Milford laughed as she remembered this.

"There you are! It makes you laugh to remember it!"

"I didn't laugh at the time. I cried for hours."

"I bet when I'm as old as you," said Etta, "and I try to remember when I was little I won't be able to think of a single thing to laugh at. It'll all seem the same. All dull and . . . like years and years of cold cereal!"

"Oh, Etta! I'm sure it won't be like that."

"You don't know what it's like," said Etta fiercely. "You had a sister and two brothers!"

She had worked herself up into such a state by this time that she felt she couldn't stay indoors any longer. She ran out of the kitchen and down the garden to the shed where her bicycle was kept. Ten minutes later she was cycling hard along the smooth concrete promenade down by the sea, paying no attention to the sign that said "Bicycles Forbidden," nor of the scowls and complaints of the old ladies walking their poodles and scotties.

When her legs began to feel weary with pedaling she left her bicycle on the promenade and went down onto the beach to hurl pebbles at the stupid gray-green sea. It was almost an hour later when she finally turned toward home. She realized how late it was when she saw that the car was in the garage, and that meant her father was home from work.

3 . A Sort of Brother

In fact they had begun to eat without her.

"Yours is in the oven," said her mother. "Be careful you don't burn yourself."

Etta brought her plate to the table and sat up. She knew that they were both looking hard at her, but she pretended not to notice. She began to eat. "Um! My favorite," she said, crunching the crackly edge of the crust.

There was a long silence. She knew that they had been talking about her and that they were now having a silent argument by nodding and making faces at each other. She looked up quickly and caught them at it. They both looked down at their plates and her father made a noise a bit like a cough and a bit like a laugh. Then he put his knife and fork down and wiped his lips with his napkin.

"We've been talking about you," he said.

Etta went on eating but gave a little nod to show she was listening.

"About you being a lonely only," he added.

There was another silence and he coughed once or twice. "We've talked about it many times before," he said, "but it's never got us anywhere. What we've been wondering is . . . whether you really would like it if there were another member of the family. . . ."

Etta sat very still. She felt that if she even blinked, it

would all go wrong. She had strange shivery feelings going up and down her back.

"I mean," her father stumbled on, "it's one of those things that once you've done you can't go back on. You can't suddenly change your mind. Are you sure you'd like it if you had a brother or sister?"

Etta looked up. She didn't dare speak, so she nodded, very fiercely, two or three times.

"You see," said her mother, "although I can't have another baby—and anyway, a baby would be too young for you to play with, wouldn't it—we could adopt someone. But you'd have to be very, very sure you wanted us to."

"I'm very, very sure," said Etta, hardly able to get the words out.

Her father and mother looked at each other across the table. Etta didn't dare look up to see. Her father picked up his knife and fork again.

"Well, then," he said. "We'll have to find out more about it, won't we?"

Etta found out during the next two or three days that nothing ever happens when you want it to. In fact, sometimes the more you want a thing to happen, the longer it takes, as if it were being awkward on purpose. Every time she asked her father he said that he had been in touch with somebody or other or he had been making inquiries or that he was waiting for an answer to some letter or other.

"It's not like buying something from a shop," Mr. Milford said, when Etta was worrying him for the umpteenth time. "You can't just ride up and say, "I want to adopt a nice nine-year-old girl because my daughter is a lonely only. And please can I have one with fair hair and blue eyes and a good temper.""

"Boy," said Etta.

"What?"

"Boy. Girls are silly. I want you to adopt a boy."

"Oh," said Mr. Milford. "I naturally thought . . . um . . . I wonder if that's a good idea?"

"Mum said she always wanted a baby boy," said Etta. "So that's two against one."

"Yes," said Mr. Milford. "Well, we'll just have to see, won't we?"

But they didn't see anything for the next day or so, for nothing whatever happened. Etta became very moody. She moped about even more than usual. She spent a lot of time imagining to herself what this new brother would be like. He would be tall and thin, of course, even taller than she was. He would have very fair hair that flopped over his face when he laughed. He would be a very fast runner, good at climbing, and he would have lots of brilliant ideas about things to do. She couldn't decide whether his eyes ought to be gray or green like her own. Perhaps gray would be better.

A week had passed and then Mr. Milford had a letter with *County Council Children's Department* printed in black on the outside of the envelope.

"This will be news at last," he said, opening it. And then when he'd read it he passed it across to his wife.

"Well?" said Etta. "What does it say? Yes or no?"

"Neither," said her mother. "It says that a Miss Mallim from the Children's Department is going to call on us."

"What for?" asked Etta.

Mrs. Milford made a sort of sniffing noise. "I guess she's going to look us over and see if we're suitable."

"Well," said Mr. Milford, "they'd have to do something of the sort, wouldn't they?"

"I suppose so," said Mrs. Milford. "All the same, why *Miss* Mallim? Probably some chit of a girl straight from college who thinks she knows everything and has never had to try to do a full-time job, bring up a family, and run a house all in twenty-four hours a day."

Mr. Milford laughed. "You don't know."

His wife snorted. "No, I don't know. But I wouldn't mind having a bet. Well, come on, both of you. I want to have this house spotless before she arrives and you'll both have to help me."

Mr. Milford groaned. He hated housework. "I was going to mow the lawn this evening," he said.

"It can wait," said Mrs. Milford. "And you might make a start on those tiles in the bathroom. There are three of them now that have come away from the wall."

"I don't have any cement," said Mr. Milford.

Mrs. Milford looked at the clock. "Then you'd better hurry and get some before the shops close," she said briskly. "Come on, Etta. Vacuuming is your job to start."—

The whole of that evening the house was a bustle of activity, with Mrs. Milford driving them all without mercy. When Etta or her father finished a job and sank exhausted into a chair for a few minutes, she was sure to pounce on them with something else that needed doing. Around half-past eight Mr. Milford made a feeble effort at rebellion.

"There's a good play on television tonight," he said. "Cavan Kendall's in it; you know how much you like him."

"Surely we can do without television for one night?" said Mrs. Milford. "The living-room windows are abso-

lutely filthy. Have a stab at them before it gets dark, will
you? Oh, and Etta! Your rabbit's hutch needs cleaning
out. It stinks to high heaven."

Etta and her father looked at each other, laughed hys-
terically and then went about their new tasks.

But when Etta opened up the hutch, her mood changed
right away. The hutch was filthy, no doubt about it. During the last week she had not paid much attention to it.
"Poor Gretel," she said. "I've been neglecting you, haven't
I?"

Gretel the rabbit twitched its nose and then thumped
its back legs emphatically.

"You're quite right," said Etta. "I'm a wicked, lazy girl.
I think you'd better go for a little run in the garden while I
clean up."

She picked up the rabbit and put it down on the edge of the lawn, where it nibbled a few blades of grass and then made off in long hops toward the vegetable patch by the shed.

"Please! Please!" called Etta. "Don't eat those little lettuce plants, like you did last time."

The rabbit didn't seem to hear, for it made straight for the row of new plants. Etta watched with a worried expression as Gretel neatly nipped off the first lettuce close to the ground and then sat back chewing her way through it. When the last edge of green had disappeared and a second lettuce was nipped off, Etta sighed. "Well, just one or two, then," she said. "Perhaps Dad will think it's slugs or birds or something."

She cleaned the hutch out as quickly as she could, put down clean sawdust and some fresh hay and then went to look for Gretel. Nearly half of the young lettuces were gone.

"Where are you?" said Etta. "Gretel! You're a very naughty girl!"

The rabbit sat up and looked at her. It was now among the ferny leaves of the new carrots.

Etta snatched it up and stared down at the damage. Half a dozen carrots showed bright-orange patches where they had been nibbled.

"That's very wasteful," Etta told her. "Nobody would mind if you just ate one, but you've spoiled lots. And also," she added, "you've left your silly teeth marks on them so that anyone can tell it was you that did it!"

She gave the rabbit a shake to show that she was cross and then gave it a hug to show that it had been forgiven.

"There," she said, putting it back in the hutch, "what do you say to me for cleaning out your hutch so nicely?"

The rabbit didn't say anything but started to nibble the clean hay.

Etta sighed. "Now I'd better break the bad news to Dad," she said. "Get it over as soon as possible."

Indoors Mr. Milford was stretched out in an armchair looking absolutely exhausted. "I'm on strike," he said when Etta came in. "Your mother wants all the rugs changed around."

"Not all of them," said Mrs. Milford, coming in at that moment. "Only two. The one in our bedroom is much better than this old thing. I've been wanting to switch them for months. It'll only take a few minutes."

Etta said, "I'm afraid Gretel has been rather naughty again, Dad."

"Oh, dear. What's she done this time?"

"Never mind the rabbit," said Mrs. Milford. "Are you going to help me with these carpets?"

"I told you, I'm on strike," said Mr. Milford.

Surprisingly Mrs. Milford gave in. She sat down, looked at the rug and then leaned back in the chair looking quite worn out. "I suppose it's not too bad," she said.

Mr. Milford got up. "At last," he said. "Now you sit there and rest for a while and I'll go and fix us all a nice hot drink."

He went off into the kitchen, so Etta sat down thinking how lucky she was not to have any fuss about Gretel. Of course, he'd probably blow up when he saw his baby lettuces, but at least she had tried to tell him.

"Mum," she said, after they had been sitting in silence for a while. "Can we call him Kevin?"

"Call who Kevin?"

"The boy we're going to adopt."

"He'll have a name already."

"I hadn't thought of that." Etta thought of it now.

"I do hope we're doing the right thing," said Mrs. Milford. "It's a dreadful responsibility."

"Suppose we don't like him?" said Etta.

"Suppose he doesn't like us!"

"That's silly," said Etta. "He's bound to like us."

"It's not silly. There's no rule about liking people."

Etta began to worry about this. Although she got along very well at school and was quite popular, there were three or four children in her class who didn't like her at all. She tried to imagine what it would be like having one of those to live with them. She shuddered at the thought. "Well," she said, "we'd just have to send him back, that's all."

Mr. Milford came in with three mugs. "Couldn't find any cocoa," he said. "I've made malteds. Hope that pleases everyone."

They were both pleased and said so.

"And what's all this about sending someone back?" he asked.

"This boy," said Etta. "If we didn't like him or if he didn't like us."

Mr. Milford grunted and sipped at his drink. "If we're going to start off by thinking of how we can get out of it perhaps it would be better to stop right now."

"Oh, no!" cried Etta.

"What I mean," said Mr. Milford, "is that whoever we take on is bound to be a bit unhappy to start with. And it'll be hard for him to come into a family that he doesn't know. It will take him a long time to get used to our funny ways."

"I haven't got any funny ways," said Etta indignantly.

Both parents burst out laughing at this. "Not much!" said her father.

"I haven't. I'm just ordinary. I bet you can't tell me anything funny I do!"

"We'd be here till midnight if I did start," said her father.

Mrs. Milford, suddenly reminded of the time, looked at the clock and jumped up. "Past nine!" she exclaimed, "and you still up. Come on, young lady. Bedtime. And quick about it!"

4 . Enter Miss Mallim

The front-door bell rang as the hall clock was striking six. Etta started toward the door.

"No," said her mother. "That'll be Miss Mallim. I'll go. Your father would be late tonight of all nights."

"He's not late yet," said Etta. "He hardly ever gets in before ten past."

Mrs. Milford gave a last despairing look around and hurried to the door.

"Apron," said Etta.

Mrs. Milford snatched her apron off and pushed it out of sight under a cushion. Etta heard the voices in the hall as the door was opened.

"Mrs. Milford?"

"Yes, that's right. Won't you come in?"

"Thank you. I—"

"You're Miss Mallim from the Children's Department, aren't you? My husband isn't back yet, but I don't think he'll be very long. That's right, in here."

Etta thought Miss Mallim was pretty. She was very tall with very long legs. She had streaky hair, very fair on top but darker underneath where the sun didn't reach. Everything about her was long—her face, her arms, even her fingers. She had a way of flicking her fingers, as if she had touched something sticky. And she kept her arms bent with

33

her hands just in front of her, as if she didn't like them to hang down so far away. She was wearing a very pale blue linen dress with white buttons all the way down the front.

"This is my daughter Etta," said Mrs. Milford. "Short for Henrietta."

"That's nice," said Miss Mallim and shook hands with Etta. Then her face suddenly took on a worried expression. "That's something I ought to have thought of," she said, half to herself. "Is everyone tall in this family?"

"Etta takes after her grandfather," said Mrs. Milford. "Mr. Milford is more what you'd call stocky, as you'll see when he comes in. Why do you ask?"

"It's only that . . ." Miss Mallim began and then hesitated. "You did say your husband would be home soon, didn't you?"

"In a few minutes, I imagine."

"We don't want to say everything twice, do we?" She turned to Etta and started asking her questions about school and her friends and how she got along with the teachers. Mrs. Milford muttered something about a cup of tea and hurried out.

After a while Miss Mallim sat looking thoughtfully at the bowl of flowers in the window and Etta tried to think of something to talk about.

"Would you like me to show you over the house?" she asked at last. "I mean, you want to inspect it, don't you?"

Miss Mallim laughed.

"I did the vacuuming," Etta said. "Under the beds and everything. It'll be an awful waste if you don't come and look at it."

"I think we'll wait and see what your mother says." Miss Mallim seemed very amused about something. She kept chuckling to herself, then trying to look serious and then chuckling again. Etta gave up. "Well, at least," she said, "you can come and look at my rabbit, I suppose. We don't need permission to do that."

"I'd like to see your rabbit," said Miss Mallim.

Etta took her out and showed her the hutch and took Gretel out so that she could be looked at properly. She told Miss Mallim about Gretel's misbehavior among the lettuces and carrots. As they were going back in, Miss Mallim told her about a pet goat she'd had when she was a girl and how it was always getting her into trouble by eating the shoots off the roses.

Etta's father had come home by now, and they all sat around drinking tea and talking about nothing in particular for what seemed hours. Etta could not understand why they didn't get on with it. If Miss Mallim had come to talk about the boy they were going to adopt, why didn't she say something about it? Etta managed to eat three chocolate cookies before her mother noticed and frowned at her, but otherwise it was very boring.

"Clear the cups, will you, Etta?" said Mrs. Milford. "And then go and watch television for a while, or read, or something. We want to have a quiet talk with Miss Mallim."

"You're trying to get rid of me," Etta accused.

"Well, yes, in a way. But we'll tell you all about it later. I promise."

"If you're going to tell me afterward, why can't I stay now?"

"Do as I say. Be a good girl."

Etta gave one of her highest shrugs and then began to clear the cups. In the kitchen she even washed them and put the things away, all the time grumbling aloud to herself. She thought she deserved another chocolate cookie after that.

There was nothing very interesting on television, so she started to read, but all the time she was wondering what they were talking about in the living room. In the end she went quietly down the passage and stood outside the door. She recognized Miss Mallim's voice.

". . . and the other one is a boy named Paul Aintree, who came into our care about three years ago when his mother died. Nothing is known about his father."

"How old is he?" asked Mrs. Milford.

"He'd be seven and a half—going on eight."

"That's rather young, isn't it? We'd been thinking of someone more Etta's age. . . ."

"I'm sorry," said Miss Mallim. "We couldn't recommend a boy of the same age. There are many reasons. In the first place . . ."

She went on to explain to Mr. and Mrs. Milford, but Etta could not understand what she was talking about and in the end she drifted away back to the television set. "Paul Aintree, Paul Aintree," she said over and over to herself a few times. Somehow she could not fit her picture of a tall, fair boy to the name of Paul. "And anyway," she thought, "if he's not eight yet, he'll only be a little kid, like those noisy boys at school that rush around the playground pretending to be Superman, or Batman, or an airplane or spaceman, or something childish like that."

After a while it occurred to her that if he was younger than she was at least he wouldn't be able to boss her around. That cheered her up a little, but not much.

Half an hour later she heard voices in the hall and the bang of the front door, so she guessed Miss Mallim had gone. She went through to see what her parents had to say. They were both looking depressed.

"Well?" said Etta.

Her father heaved a deep sigh and made an effort to rouse himself. "Yes," he said. "Well, I'm not sure where to start."

"Begin at the beginning, go on to the end and then stop," said Etta.

Her father laughed. "Easier said than done. It's turned out to be a hundred times more complicated than we thought."

"We didn't expect it to be as easy as buying a can of baked beans," said Mrs. Milford.

"No, of course not, but all these forms and inquiries and waiting periods and trial periods and doctor's certificates and—"

Etta interrupted. "What I want to know is, are we going to have someone or not?"

"They won't let us adopt a boy of your age, at least not right away," said her father. "But we can have a boy living with us. We'd be the foster parents."

"What's the difference?" said Etta. "It doesn't matter much what people call it. As long as he's living with us."

"There is a difference, though. It's not permanent. The real parents can always ask for him back."

"But his mother's dead," said Etta.

"How do you know that?"

"I listened at the door for a while," said Etta guiltily.

"That wasn't very nice."

"Well, you shouldn't have sent me out. I wanted to know what was happening. Anyway, I didn't hear much. I couldn't understand half of what Miss Mallim was saying."

"What else did you hear?"

"Nothing really. Except that his name is Paul Aintree."

"Well," said her father, "there's no harm done. Actually

she mentioned two boys, but she thought I ought to see Paul first. I'll be going down to Magsted to see him on Saturday afternoon."

"Why can't he just come here?"

"We don't even know that he would want to. It's all got to be done gradually. Miss Mallim said she thought it would be best if we had him to dinner once or twice and then to see how things went."

Etta sighed. "It's all so slow," she said.

"Better slow than sorry," said her mother.

"Why do you have to go to Magsted? That's miles away."

"Paul is in a children's home there."

"Can I come with you on Saturday?"

Mr. Milford looked doubtful. "Miss Mallim said the fewer the better first time."

Etta's mother said, "I'd think it would make it easier for you. After all, a boy that age might easily be frightened of a strange man. But someone more his own age . . ."

Mr. Milford looked offended. "Well, that's nice," he said. "Anyone would think I went around terrifying the life out of all the children I meet."

"Of course I didn't mean that."

Etta waited for an answer to her question. Her father thought about it for quite a long time. "Yes, all right," he said at last. "You can come with me."

5 . Visitors

Paul and Sadi had been trying for weeks to swim a length of the pool. On this particular Saturday morning they finally succeeded and ran triumphant down to the office to tell Mr. Truman, the Superintendent, because when anybody swam a length for the first time he could have his name written up on the big board in the hall.

Mr. Truman noted their names. "Well done," he said. "I'll write your names in next time I go up to the hall. Oh, by the way, Sadi, I had a phone call from your mother. She's coming down tomorrow afternoon and would like to take you out to dinner."

Sadi looked pleased. Her mother was a nurse who worked in a hospital in London, and she did not often get time to come down and see Sadi. The last time had been a month ago.

"Oh, and Paul," he went on. "I wonder if you'd do me a favor. A friend of mine is coming this afternoon and I said I'd show him around. But in fact I'll be too busy. Would you mind doing it for me?"

"Me?" said Paul. "Why not one of the older ones? I'm not much good at showing people things."

"I'd like you to do it," said Mr. Truman. "That's why I asked you. But if it's too much trouble I can probably find someone else."

Paul didn't really want the job, but he was pleased that Mr. Truman wanted him to do it. "All right," he said. "I don't mind."

"His name's Mr. Milford," said Mr. Truman. "And he may be bringing his daughter with him. She'd be about your age or a bit older. He's a nice chap; you'll like him. He said he'd be coming soon after lunch. I'll call you when I need you."

They went back up to the house to get changed out of their swimming things, and by that time it was almost midday. As it was Paul's day for setting the tables he went down to the common room to get it done, and when Sadi offered to help him, he let her.

"Are you afraid I'll push you over again?" she said.

Paul laughed, remembering how bad-tempered he had been that morning.

While they were setting the table Jock came in with a package that had just been sent up for him from the office. He came slowly into the common room with it, looking at the label with his name and address on it.

"What is it?" asked Paul.

"I haven't got X-ray eyes," said Jock.

"I guess it's a birthday present," said Sadi.

"Brilliant deduction," said Jock. "Seeing as it's my birthday tomorrow. It's my father's writing on the label. That's all I can say about it."

"Well, open it!" said Paul.

"No, you mustn't," said Sadi. "You must keep it till the proper day."

"I don't want it at all," said Jock. Suddenly he thrust the package at Paul. "Here you are. You have it. Happy birthday!"

"But you can't do that," said Paul. "You don't even know what it is. And anyway, it's a present from your father."

"He's joking," said Sadi.

"I'm not," said Jock grimly. "I don't want a present from my father. He hasn't been to see me for two years. I don't know why he bothers to send me a present at all. Anyway I don't want it!" He flung the present across the room and it fell on the floor behind one of the armchairs.

"I guess he doesn't have much time to come and see you," said Sadi. "Perhaps he lives too far away."

"Ha, ha, ha!" said Jock in a hollow voice. Then he thrust his hands deep into his pockets and walked out of the room.

When he had gone, Paul said to Sadi, "He was crying, wasn't he?"

She nodded.

"What do you think we ought to do about the package?"

"Nothing," she said. "Just leave it there. He might change his mind. He might open it later when he's by himself."

A few minutes later Rosine was banging the gong in the hall and the children began to troop in for the meal.

Afterward some of the older boys wanted to have a ball game and they were trying to talk the younger ones into joining them. When they asked Paul he said, "You only want me to play so that I can run around and get the ball for you."

"No, honest. We'll let you have a turn batting," they said.

"Which ball are you playing with?"

"The real one, of course. You're not frightened of a hard ball, are you?"

Paul was, but didn't like to admit it. "I've got to do a job for Mr. Truman anyway," he said.

"You're just saying that."

"No he's not," said Sadi. "I was there when Mr. Truman asked him. He's going to show someone around."

"You could play till he wants you."

Paul was trying to think of a way out when fortunately a little girl came up from the office to say Mr. Truman wanted him.

"There you are!" he said. "I told you, didn't I?"

Mr. Truman's office was rather small, and when Paul got there it seemed to be full of people.

"Ah, Paul," said Mr. Truman. "Now this is Mr. Milford, the friend I was talking about."

A short, stocky man who had been sitting in the visitor's chair got up and offered Paul his hand. Paul noticed how hairy it was. A fierce dark forest of hair sprouted out of the back of his hand and a fringe of hair stuck out below his shirt cuff. Paul liked him immediately.

"And this is Etta," went on Mr. Truman, waving his hand toward a long, thin girl leaning awkwardly against the cabinet. She had been staring at Paul ever since he came in but now, when he turned to look at her, she looked away quickly and fixed her eyes on the calendar which had a picture of a lake and some mountains. Paul looked at her long enough to see she had pale skin with freckles on her nose, a narrow pointed chin, and eyes that were probably green.

"Whenever you're ready," said Mr. Milford.

Paul felt rather lost. He had never shown anyone over the Home before, and he wasn't at all sure what to do. Mr. Truman must have guessed this because he told Paul where to take them and gave him various keys from the board so that he could open some of the doors that were kept locked.

The path through the woods from the office was fairly narrow. Paul and Mr. Milford walked together, Etta trailed some distance behind, touching tree trunks as she passed.

"I gather from Mr. Truman that you haven't been here very long," Mr. Milford said.

"Not long," Paul agreed.

"Do you like it here?"

It seemed an odd question, and Paul didn't know how to answer. "It's all right," he said.

Mr. Milford seemed to understand. "I suppose what I really meant was do you like it better than the place you were at before? Mr. Truman told us you were with foster parents. . . ."

"Oh, that!" said Paul. "It's much better here."

"Why?"

"I don't know. It just is. Where I was before they were all mad. They kept fighting all the time."

Etta giggled when he said this. He turned around but she was already looking away through the trees.

"It wasn't funny, though," said Paul. "I used to be frightened. They really fought. They even threw things at each other."

"The other children?"

"No, the parents. Mr. and Mrs. Goodman, they were called. The people who were supposed to be looking after me. Once he knocked her down and she hit her head on the table. She was on the floor and we all thought she was dead. All the kids were crying. But someone reported him to the police and then they took me away and I came here."

Etta spoke for the first time. "I wasn't laughing at that," she said. "It was because you said about them being mad and I thought like in *Alice*—the March Hare and the Hatter and all saying funny things and putting butter in the watch to make it go better."

Paul grinned. "That wouldn't have been so bad," he said. "But they weren't ever funny mad, just frightening mad."

They had reached the house where he lived, so he took them in and showed them over it. When they got upstairs he showed them where he slept. Etta picked up the photograph that stood on the table by his bed.

"That's my Mum," he said. "She's dead."

"She's very pretty," Etta said. "What color hair did she have?"

Paul looked at the picture as if seeing it for the first time. "I don't remember," he said. "It was a long time ago."

Etta put the picture back and then sat on the bed, bouncing and testing the springs. She looked around the room. "Six beds," she said.

"Six boys in this house," Paul said. "And four girls. Their room is across the landing. You'd better see that too. They keep theirs neater than we do."

The four girls' beds had yellow bedspreads and there was a pattern of flying birds on the wallpaper. Etta thought it was lovely and said so.

"It's all right," said Paul. He couldn't see why it was any better than the boys' room. "That's my friend's bed over by the window. Her mother's a nurse in London."

Etta looked at the photographs, which were mostly of Sadi and her mother together. She didn't say anything about them. She looked out of the window. "What's that plank thing going through the trees?"

"It's the tree-walk. It's my favorite of all the things here," Paul said. "And the swimming pool is the next best."

"Will you show us?" asked Mr. Milford.

Paul showed them the tree-walk and they all three climbed up and walked around it. He showed them the swimming pool.

"I swam a length this morning," he said.

"Well done," said Mr. Milford.

"I can't swim at all," said Etta.

By this time Paul found that he could talk quite easily to Mr. Milford and was getting on fairly well with Etta, although she puzzled him. He had the odd feeling that she was disappointed about something, and that in some way he was to blame. Perhaps he was not showing them around very well.

He told them funny stories about some of the things that happened, and he also told them about Jock and the package, and about Evelyn on the tree-walk. When Mr. Milford asked him about school, he told him what they did and what the school was like.

"What about the weekends?" said Mr. Milford. "What do you do with yourself?"

Paul tried to think, but apart from swimming with Sadi nothing much occurred to him. "Fool around," he said. "Nothing special."

"I was wondering," said Mr. Milford, "if you'd like to come to our place for dinner some time. It might make a change."

"I don't mind," said Paul. "Do you live in Magsted?"

"No. We live about twenty-five miles away."

"How would I find the place then?"

"I'd come and get you, of course."

Paul thought about this for a moment. "Is that your car by the gate? The red one?"

"Yes, that's right."

"I've never seen one like that before. What is it?"

"It's a Volvo. A Swedish car."

"All right, then," said Paul. "I'd like to come sometime."

"Well, let's fix something definite," said Mr. Milford quickly. "What about tomorrow?"

"All right . . . no it's not. It's Jock's birthday party. I don't want to miss that."

"No, of course not. Next weekend then?"

"All right."

"Saturday?"

"All right."

By this time they were almost back at the office. Paul saw Mr. Truman on the step waiting for them. "All right?" he called.

"Fine!" said Mr. Milford with enthusiasm. "Couldn't be better."

"What about you, young lady?" said Mr. Truman. "You don't look too happy."

Etta gave a feeble smile but did not answer.

Mr. Milford started to tell Mr. Truman about Paul coming to lunch with them next weekend. Mr. Truman agreed with this immediately. In fact, Paul had a strange feeling that he had known about it all along. He thought about this after he had said good-bye to Mr. Milford and Etta and was walking back to the house.

6 . Paul Goes Visiting

Mr. Milford drove toward home. Neither he nor Etta spoke for some time, then he said, "Well, come on, what's eating you?"

"Nothing," said Etta.

"Oh, yes, it is. You've got a face like a wet Sunday. What are you worrying about?"

"You'll just say I'm being silly."

"I promise not to."

Etta still hesitated. She knew in fact that she was being silly, but she couldn't help it. "Well," she said at last, "it's just that I thought he was going to be tall, like me, and with fair hair."

"Is that all?"

"I was disappointed," said Etta in a sulky voice. "I couldn't get used to him being such a shrimp."

"Well, I like that!" exclaimed her father. "I suppose you'd say I was a shrimp."

Etta laughed. "You are, really. I'll be taller than you in a few years' time. But that's different. You've always been like that. It's not the same as being disappointed."

"Do you think you'll get over it?"

"Oh, I suppose so. He's all right, really. Just different, that's all."

"I took to him right away," said Mr. Milford. "I think he liked me, too."

"That was obvious," said Etta bitterly. "But I thought we were supposed to be getting someone for me to play with."

"It's a bit more serious than that," said Mr. Milford. "The idea is to have a proper sort of family instead of only half a one."

Etta watched the moving countryside without saying anything more for quite a time, and then, as if she had settled something in her mind, she said, "I suppose it'll be all right. I did really like him. But I wonder what he thinks about it, though?"

"Who, Paul? He just thinks he's been invited out to dinner. He doesn't know about all these plans we've got. We'll have to get to know him before we say a word about his coming to live with us."

"I bet he knows all about it," said Etta.

"He doesn't. Mr. Truman was quite definite about saying nothing until we saw how things went."

"All the same, I bet he knows," said Etta darkly.

Paul had been telling Sadi about the Milfords and about his invitation to their home.

"Did you think she was pretty?" Sadi asked.

Paul considered this. "No," he said at last. "She was too skinny. She walked along the tree-walk without holding, though."

"Well so do I."

"You hold on sometimes."

"Only at the corners."

"She can't swim," said Paul.

They had been setting the table while they were talking.

This reminded Paul of the business about Jock's package, so he went and looked over the back of the armchair.

"It's still there," he said.

Sadi shrugged her shoulders. She was not interested in Jock's package; she was thinking about the Milfords. "What's her name?" she asked.

"Etta."

Sadi gave a quick laugh. "She etta big dinner," she said.

"It's no funnier than yours," Paul objected.

Jock had come downstairs and was leaning in the doorway. He still looked pretty miserable. "Well," he said, "did they invite you to their house?"

"How did you know?"

Jock grinned a twisted sort of smile. "They always do,"

he said. "As soon as I saw you showing that man around I guessed it was a fostering job."

Paul didn't understand. He looked at Sadi and she shook her head. "I don't know what you're talking about," he said.

"When you've been here as long as I have," Jock said, "you know as soon as you see them."

"Know what?"

"You know they're foster parents. It's always the same. First they ask you to dinner a few times, then you stay for the weekend, and so it goes on."

"What's wrong with that?" Paul asked.

"Nothing's wrong with it. I just said that's what happens, that's all. If you want to be fostered it's all right."

"Why didn't Mr. Truman say something to me about it?"

"How should I know?" said Jock. "You know what grown-ups are like. Half the time you can't tell why they do things."

Paul didn't ask any more questions. He ate his meal in silence and afterward he slipped out on his own and climbed up to the tree-walk. For the next half hour he walked around and around and around the high plank walk between the trees, stopping each time at the farthest-distant point, where it was possible to look down into Mr. Truman's garden. It was a warm evening and Mr. Truman was stretched out in a deck chair reading. The sound of music came from the open windows.

Paul had a very lonely feeling. He thought he would go down and ask Mr. Truman if what Jock had said was true. Then he changed his mind and went back to the house. In the common room they were watching television. He stood at the door for a few minutes and then turned away and went up to the bedroom. It was empty. He slowly got undressed and climbed into bed, where he pulled the covers right over his head.

Later Rosine came through the bedroom and saw his shape in the bed. She leaned over and drew the covers back to see his face.

"Powl!" she said. "Are you ill or something?"

Paul turned over with his face away from her. He dragged the cover back over his face and held it tight with both hands.

"Never mind," she said gently and patted his shoulder. "You sleep now and tomorrow maybe you forget all about it, eh?"

"Fat lot you know," Paul muttered to himself when she had gone.

He did fall asleep very soon, but all night long he had horrible, frightening dreams.

The following Saturday Mr. Milford arrived at the Home early in the afternoon to collect Paul.

"You're looking very nice," he said as Paul climbed into the front seat.

Paul scowled. "Rosine made me put these clothes on," he complained. "Just like going to church. I hate wearing a tie anyway."

Mr. Milford laughed. "That makes two of us," he said.

They drove for some time without speaking. Paul wanted to ask Mr. Milford if it was true that the Milfords wanted to foster him, but every time he got ready to ask, something stopped him. He looked around for something else to say and his eye fell on the radio.

"Is that the radio?" he asked. Mr. Milford would think him pretty stupid asking a question like that.

"You can turn it on if you like," Mr. Milford said.

Paul shook his head. "No, thank you," he said.

They drove a little farther without either of them speaking. Mr. Milford hummed a tune under his breath, then he said, "How did Jock's birthday party go?"

"All right" said Paul. "It was a good party. Rosine made jellies and cakes and everything."

"Did Jock get lots of presents?"

"I don't think so. Some of the boys he's friends with gave him pens and things like that. And Mr. Truman gave him a football. Mr. Truman gives everyone a present when it's their birthday."

"What about the package from his father?"

"Jock wouldn't open it. He threw it away in the garbage pail without even cutting the string."

"That's sad," said Mr. Milford. "And a waste, too."

"That's what Rosine said. So Jock said she could have it if she liked and she got it out of the pail and it was a big paintbox. Not a kids' one but the sort grown-ups use. Rosine put it in the common room for anyone to paint with, but nobody has so far."

"Why's that?"

"I don't know. Just don't like to, I suppose."

"Not far now," said Mr. Milford a little later. "You'll be able to see the sea when we get around the next bend."

"I didn't know you lived near the sea," said Paul.

"Very close, as a matter of fact. A couple of years ago a very high tide carried away part of our garden fence. Now look! There it is."

They were going down a fairly steep hill and straight in

front Paul could see the gray-green of the water. "Imagine living so near the sea and not being able to swim," he said.

Mr. Milford laughed. "Etta, you mean? She never stays in long enough to learn. I guess it's because she's so thin. Thin people get cold quickly."

They were in the town now, through narrow streets filled with cars. Mr. Milford drove slowly, stopping every few yards because of the traffic. "That's the harbor," he said, nodding to the left. "You might like to poke around there."

Paul caught a glimpse of two ships quite close to the road, of tall cranes, trucks, heaps of sand and stones, and rusty iron structures built high into the air. Then the car swung suddenly up a turning among tall trees, then up a sharp concrete ramp and into a garage, stopping a couple of inches from the back wall.

Mr. Milford laughed at the look on Paul's face. "Sorry," he said. "I've done it so often. That must have given you rather a shock."

Paul grinned. "Is this where you live?"

"Well, it's where the car lives. We live in the house," said Mr. Milford.

Paul didn't think this was very funny but he laughed just the same. They got out and Mr. Milford led the way through the door at the back of the garage. There was a small garden, mostly grass surrounded by trees, a climbing frame and a swing, and beyond the fence at the end was the sea again.

"It is near, isn't it?" said Paul. "I ought to have brought my swimming trunks."

"You must remember next time you come," said Mr. Milford.

Paul was reminded of what Jock had said and immediately felt awkward again. "I don't want to swim in it much," he said. "It looks dirty."

"Oh," said Mr. Milford, taken by surprise. "Well, we'll see, won't we?"

They entered the house through a side door that led straight into the kitchen. Mr. Milford shouted out, "We're home," as soon as they were inside the door.

"We're at the back!" came an answering shout.

"Follow me, and don't get lost on the way," said Mr. Milford cheerfully. "People have died of starvation in this house, trying to find their way out without a compass."

It wasn't really that complicated, but the rooms were oddly arranged and led into one another so that you could

go right around in a circle. They arrived at the end room, which was the one with a television set in and the French windows leading out into the garden again. Mrs. Milford and Etta were watching tennis.

"So this is Paul!" said Mrs. Milford. "Hello!"

Paul smiled at her. He thought she looked rather nice. Then he looked at Etta, but she had her eyes fixed on the screen and didn't look up. Mrs. Milford went over to the set and switched it off.

"Oh, Mum!" wailed Etta. "It was just at the most exciting part. Turn it on again, quick!"

"Not now, dear."

"It's the championship! Don't you understand?" shouted Etta rudely. She jumped up and went toward the set as if she were going to turn it on herself.

"Etta!" said Mr. Milford sharply. "Leave the set alone. Behave yourself!"

Etta turned on Paul, who had stood amazed. "It's all your fault!" she said, and then stamped out of the room and slammed the door behind her.

"Well!" exclaimed Mrs. Milford. "Don't pay any attention, Paul. She gets these tempers sometimes. She'll come back and say she's sorry in a minute."

"She certainly will!" declared Mr. Milford angrily and left the room.

Paul didn't know what to say, so he kept quiet. Mrs. Milford started asking him questions, about the Home and his friends there, and seemed very interested when he told her about Sadi and Jock and the twins and Evelyn and the others.

"But you don't have a mother or a father, do you?" she said.

"No," said Paul.

"I guess you get pretty lonely sometimes."

Paul was going to tell her about being lonely, but then he changed his mind and said, "I'm all right. There are always plenty of people at the Home."

Mrs. Milford gave him rather an odd look, as if she didn't believe him, and then she changed the subject and started asking him whether he liked bananas and custard and so on. In the middle of this Etta came back.

She came in, closed the door gently behind her, and leaned on it looking down at her shoes.

"Well, dear?" said Mrs. Milford.

"I'm sorry I was so beastly," mumbled Etta.

"I think it's Paul you should apologize to."

Etta just glanced up long enough to see that Paul was looking at her. "I'm sorry I said it was all your fault," she mumbled.

"All right," said Paul.

Mrs. Milford got up. "Well, if you two could amuse yourselves for a little while, I'll go and get dinner," she said.

As soon as she had gone and the door had closed behind her, Etta said to Paul, "Do you like tennis?"

"I never watched it," he said.

"Do you mind if I just watch the rest of the match?"

"What about your mother? Won't she be angry?"

"I'll turn the sound down. If you don't want to watch, you can have a try at the climbing frame."

"All right," said Paul.

So he went out through the French windows and climbed around on the climbing frame while Etta crouched over the silent television set with one hand on the knob, ready to switch it off if she heard anyone coming. When Mrs. Milford called them both in about twenty minutes later, the tennis match was over and both children were playing in the garden very happily. Paul was showing Etta how he could hang by his toes from the top bar of the frame.

"Oh, my goodness!" exclaimed Mrs. Milford. "What happens if you slip?"

"I fall on my head," said Paul cheerfully. "I did it quite a lot when I was practicing, but I don't slip now. I've got the knack of it."

The rest of the day was very successful. Mrs. Milford had prepared a splendid party, almost good enough for a birthday party. Etta was in a very friendly mood, probably because she had got her own way over the tennis match. In fact, Paul enjoyed himself and was very sorry when Mr. Milford said it was time to take him back.

"Why can't he stay the night?" said Etta.

"We'd have to ask Mr. Truman about that."

"You could call him up."

"No," said Mr. Milford. "Not this time. And anyway, we don't know if Paul would like it."

"You'd like to stay, wouldn't you, Paul?" said Etta.

"Yes," said Paul, not really sure but pleased that she wanted him to.

"We'll try and fix it another time," said Mr. Milford. "Next weekend, perhaps. I'll see Mr. Truman and ask him. Is that all right, Paul?"

"Yes," Paul said. He would have liked to ask if Sadi could come as well, but he didn't quite know how to put it.

7 . Trailer Vacation

A month later the Milfords took Paul away with them on vacation. By this time he had been three times to their house and stayed for two weekends. Paul had also met some of Etta's aunts and uncles and cousins and one or two of her school friends. He was beginning to feel quite at home in the Milfords' house.

Now it was August. It was vacation time and the Milfords were taking their trailer for two weeks to Wiltshire and Somerset.

"Have you ever been there, Paul?" asked Mr. Milford.

"I don't think so."

"Well, now's your chance. Would you like to come with us?"

And so it had been fixed up. Mr. Truman had talked to Paul about it to make sure he really wanted to go, and when Paul had said he was sure he did, Mr. Truman had seemed very pleased. Mrs. Truman packed all his clothes in a suitcase. "Have you said good-bye to everybody?" she asked.

"They all know I'm going," Paul said.

"Of course. You'd better say good-bye to Rosine, though, at least. She'd feel hurt if you didn't."

Paul went up to the house and found Rosine busy as usual. She was upstairs scrubbing out the bathroom.

"Those twins!" she said. "They wanted to play with boats in the bath. I must be mad to let them. Look at the floor! You could swim on it!"

"I'm going away for a vacation," said Paul.

"So you are. Have a good time, won't you?" She gave him a quick hug and kissed his cheek. "Off you go then. I'll make you a special cake for when you come back."

"Don't put any of that peel in it," Paul said.

"I know how you like it," she said.

He went downstairs and looked in the common room. Most of the children were in there. "I'm going in a trailer," he said.

"Lucky you," said Jock.

They all said the same sort of thing.

"Where's Sadi?" Paul asked.

"She ran into the woods," said one of the girls.

"Why?"

No one knew. "I think she was crying," said Jock.

"What about?" Paul asked.

"How should I know? Girls cry about nothing."

Paul hesitated. "Well, good-bye, then," he said and went back down to the office. A few minutes later Mr. Milford arrived to collect him and off they went.

Mrs. Milford and Etta had already packed up and were sitting waiting for them.

"You said there was a trailer," said Paul.

They explained to him that they would pick the trailer up later, on the way. It was on a farm in Sussex where they sometimes went for weekends. They would spend the first night there and then take the trailer on with them. It was quite simple really.

Paul did not understand what they were saying. It didn't seem at all simple to him. He had expected to go for a vacation in a trailer and now they were setting out without one. Suddenly he didn't want to go at all; he wanted to go back to the Home.

Mr. and Mrs. Milford looked at each other over his head with raised eyebrows. Mr. Milford started to explain again, but Paul shouted angrily, "Shut up! I don't want you to tell me all over again. I want to go home. Take me home!"

"He's just showing off," said Etta.

Paul turned and punched her as hard as he could. Etta ran off crying.

"Now look what you've done! That was very unkind. . . ."

"I don't care. I want to go home."

"Well," said Mr. Milford, "there's no need to go anywhere this very moment. I think what we all need is a little time to cool off. I vote we all relax and have a nice cool drink and a cookie. Later on we can decide what to do."

Etta seemed to have disappeared to her bedroom. Mrs. Milford went to the kitchen. Mr. Milford stretched out in an armchair and began to read his newspaper. Paul glared at him for a while, but as he didn't seem to notice he wandered sulkily off. He went from room to room banging doors and stamping his feet noisily as he went. He opened Etta's bedroom door and looked in. She was lying on her bed reading and sucking her thumb. She took her thumb out long enough to say, "Get out!" to him and then went on reading. Paul knew that he was supposed to say he was sorry for punching her but he wasn't going to because he thought she deserved it. Anyway, he wasn't sorry. She was horrible.

Mrs. Milford called up the stairs. "All right, children. Drinks ready."

Paul was in the bathroom turning the water on and off. He heard Etta going downstairs.

"Paul! Did you hear me?"

He didn't answer. After a minute he heard Etta's voice saying, "Oh, leave him alone. If he wants to go to his rotten old Home so much, why don't you take him. I don't care."

"You drink your juice and be quiet," came Mr. Milford's voice. "The trouble with you is you talk too much." He sounded angry.

Paul went on playing with the water but now he was smiling to himself. He was pleased to hear Etta being told off. Someone came up the stairs and he guessed it was Mr. Milford. He didn't look around.

"Well, young man?" demanded Mr. Milford from the bathroom door. "Did you hear Mrs. Milford calling you?"

Paul was making the soap jump into the air by squeezing it and then catching it before it splashed into the water. "Yes," he said.

"You should answer when you're called," said Mr. Milford. "Now wipe your hands and go downstairs."

Paul went on squeezing and catching.

"Did you hear me?"

"I want to go home," said Paul sulkily.

Mr. Milford suddenly lost his temper. "For two pins I'd put you across my knee and give you a good spanking," he said. "Now do as you're told this minute!"

Paul looked at him in amazement. Then he quickly washed the suds off his hands, pulled the plug out, and wiped his hands on the towel. He trotted downstairs with Mr. Milford close behind him.

"That's yours," said Mrs. Milford, pointing to a glass of juice with two shortbread cookies in a plate. Etta, already drinking her juice, glowered at him across the table.

Paul sat down. He took a drink of juice and then a bite of cookie. "What delicious juice," he said.

Etta giggled. Her parents tried to keep solemn faces.

"And delicious cookies too," said Paul.

Mr. and Mrs. Milford couldn't keep serious any longer. They both laughed. "Oh, Paul, you're dreadful," said Mrs. Milford. "You're just teasing us, aren't you?"

Ten minutes later they were all in the car happily heading west for the beginning of their vacation. And two hours later they were going slowly along a very winding lane only just wide enough for the car, with long slopes of open hillside stretching up on their left, a thick beech forest dropping down below them on their right, and not a single house in sight.

"We're nearly there, aren't we?" Etta said. "I'm sure I remember this place."

"Amazing," said her mother. "Usually you haven't the foggiest idea where we are."

The beech forest ended and just beyond it, tucked away in a hollow in the hills, was a small farmhouse with barns and farm buildings behind. Mr. Milford stopped and they all got out.

"I still can't see the trailer," Paul said.

"It's farther around the hill," said Etta. "It's in a wonderful place. Just you wait."

The farmer came out and greeted the Milfords like old friends. They all seemed to be set to gossip, so Etta asked if she could go on with Paul and show him the trailer. Mrs. Milford gave her the key and off they went.

"Don't get lost," called Mrs. Milford.

"Oh, Mum!"

"Well, you know what you are."

Paul said, "What did she mean? Do you often get lost?"

"I am sort of good at it," Etta admitted.

The lane past the farm dropped down the hillside, but Etta turned off this along a narrow footpath that kept along the side of the hill. "It's really a sheep track," she said. "Sheep are very clever at making paths that don't go up or down but keep on the same level. This one leads almost to the place."

They went out around the bulge of the hill and then up a sort of gully between two slopes. Suddenly there was the trailer, a little above them, standing on a flat grassy platform almost out of sight between two hawthorn trees.

"Isn't it a lovely place?" Etta asked.

"I don't see how you can get the car up there," said Paul.

"We don't. Mr. Sears, that's the farmer, does it for us with one of his tractors. It's a bit frightening really. When I was little I didn't dare to watch because I thought the trailer would roll over and over down the slope. Come on!"

She raced him up the last part of the slope and opened the door with the key. Paul had never been inside a trailer before and he climbed in eagerly. Everything was so neat and shiny and bright. The windows on each side looked out over miles and miles of country. The long hillsides stretched right up to the sky without a single fence. It was like being suddenly free, like a bird that goes where it wants to. He pushed a window open and the warm smell of the grass and the chorus of thousands of grasshoppers came in.

"I'd like to stay here," he said.

"We will for a day or two. It's our favorite place."

"Why not all the time?"

"Oh, you know what grown-ups are like. They like dragging around to different places. They're always stopping and walking around these old villages; that's about the worst thing. But sometimes it's all right."

"You make it sound awful."

Etta considered. "Well, it'll be better now there's two of us," she said. "Going places by yourself isn't much fun. And anyway, I said there were good parts. We go to the beach sometimes, and we might come across a circus or a fair, and there's a zoo at Bristol—"

"Where's Bristol?"

"That's a long way yet. About as far as we go usually. After Bristol the camping sites are all crowded and the roads are full of traffic and all you can smell is gasoline fumes, so we don't go."

"What's in all these cabinets?" asked Paul.

"Look and see."

Paul opened all the cabinet doors one by one and looked in. When he opened the one with pots and pans in, Etta said, "Give me the kettle. We'll have a cup of tea ready for them when they come."

Paul watched her as she poured water from a bright-blue plastic container. "There's no stove," he said. "Do we have to light a fire?"

Etta lifted up what looked like a cabinet top. "Abracadabra!" she said, and there was the stove.

"The gas tap is always too stiff for me," she said. "Come and see if you can turn it."

She showed him where the two gas bottles were on the towbar of the trailer. The taps were round knobs with arrows on to show which way you had to turn. Paul tried to turn one but it did not move at all.

"Dad always turns them off so hard," Etta said. "Never mind, we'll have to wait till they come after all."

Paul didn't like to give up. He rubbed both hands on the seat of his shorts, got a good grip with both hands on the tap, and put all his strength into the effort.

"Careful," said Etta. "Your face has turned all red and your eyes are popping out."

This made Paul laugh and he had to stop. "Don't be silly," he said. "Look the other way."

Etta turned her back and he tried again, but when she remembered what he had looked like she had to giggle and this set Paul off again.

"I'll go right away," she said. "I couldn't help it. I thought of you going off pop like a balloon."

She ran away out of sight to the other side of the trailer, but by this time Paul had the giggles himself and couldn't even get a good grip on the tap. He stopped trying for a moment, took half a dozen deep breaths, and thought of something sad to stop him from giggling. He thought of Evelyn being frightened on the tree-walk and that made him serious at once. He grasped the tap again, held his breath, and put every ounce of strength into trying to twist it.

"Ah!" he cried, letting his breath out with a rush.

Etta came running around immediately. "Now you look white as anything!" she said. "And you're sweating!"

"I turned it on, though," said Paul triumphantly, and then he suddenly went giddy and had to sit down on the grass to get over it.

"You must have strong hands," said Etta. "I can never do it, and I'm older than you."

"You're a girl, though," said Paul.

Etta was about to make a sharp reply to this when she stopped herself. After all he had turned on the tap, which was more than she could do. "You put the cups out and I'll make the tea," she said.

When Mr. and Mrs. Milford got to the trailer eventually, the children greeted them in triumph. "Come and have a cup of tea." said Etta. "Did you bring the milk?"

Mrs. Milford handed her the milk she had just got from the farmer. "However did you manage to turn the gas tap on?" she said.

"Paul did it."

"It was very easy really," said Paul.

They all looked at him with admiration.

8 . The Rough and the Smooth

That trip turned out to be pretty much as Etta had said it
would. Some parts were boring and some parts were fun.
Once or twice Paul wished he had not come, and once or
twice Etta wished there would be only one of them instead
of two. During the first two or three days they argued a
great deal and got so angry at each other that Mr. and Mrs.
Milford had to interfere and either separate them or else
quickly suggest doing something to take their minds off
their quarrel.

By the end of the week, however, they were beginning
to get used to each other. The only thing they went on
arguing about was animals. Etta was passionately fond of
every creature, big or small, and could not bear to see them
hurt or killed. Paul was very fond of the sort of animals
you could stroke or have as pets, but he couldn't understand why Etta made such a fuss about the others.

The very first day of the trip Paul was walking slowly
around on the slope near the trailer trying to find the grasshoppers that made so much noise. It was uncanny, he
thought. The sound came from all around him in a con-
tinuous chorus. There must have been thousands of them,
and yet he could not see a single grasshopper.

He knelt down on the grass to get closer, and suddenly

one jumped onto his bare knee. Paul scooped it up quickly in his hand. He could feel it, hard and shiny, pushing against the palm of his hand. It was like a tiny living bullet. Etta was down on him at once.

"Let it go!" she screeched.

"I want to look at it."

"You can look at it without holding it. Let it go!"

She was so furious that he opened his hand. The grass-hopper, bright green as if it had just been enameled, stood for a moment straightening up its legs and then took off with a sudden flick. Paul saw it land awkwardly. Then it seemed to vanish.

"I didn't get a good look at it," he complained.

Etta snorted. "I did," she said. "You must be blind if you couldn't see it."

The following day they were sitting in the trailer eating when a wasp flew in through the open window. It hovered over the jam jar but finally settled on the edge of Paul's plate, where his knife had left a smear of jam. Paul edged his hand forward and slowly picked up the knife.

"What are you going to do?" demanded Etta.

"Squash it!"

"You're not to. Dad! Tell him not to!"

"It's a wasp," said Paul. "Wasps sting people."

"They don't sting if you leave them alone."

"Well, it's eating my jam."

Mr. Milford said, "Leave it alone, Paul. It'll fly away in a moment."

"Anyway, it upsets Etta," said Mrs. Milford. "I hate wasps myself, but I know what she means. You don't have to kill things just because you don't like them."

"I think you're all silly!" said Paul. But he put the knife

down without harming the wasp and in the end it did fly away again.

"You see!" said Etta triumphantly.

"One day you'll get stung, and then you'll change your mind," said Paul.

"No, I won't," said Etta firmly. "And anyway, I have been stung, but I didn't kill the wasp. It didn't hurt for long."

"I'd kill one if it stung me," said Paul.

"I think you're horrible."

Mr. Milford looked around the trailer for some way to put an end to the argument. "Both water containers are empty," he said. "You two kids take them down to the farm while we do the dishes."

Actually they went on arguing all the way down to the farm, but when they got there they saw Mr. Sears feeding a little calf from a bottle. He let them take turns to hold the bottle, so they soon forgot about the wasp.

The following morning Mr. Sears moved the trailer down with a tractor, as Etta had said he would. He brought it right around onto the road in front of the farm and helped Mr. Milford hitch it up to the back of the Volvo.

"Right," said Mr. Milford after all the good-byes had been said. "Off we go!"

"Now comes the boring part," muttered Etta to Paul. And then to her father, "Are we going very far?"

"Don't start grumbling before we've even started," said her mother.

"I'm not grumbling, I'm asking."

"Not very far."

Etta groaned. "That's what you always say, and then we go on and on and on for ever."

"We want to get as far as Salisbury."

"How far's that?"

"About a hundred miles."

"A hundred!" Fresh groans.

They played various games for a while, like I-Spy or seeing who could see the most small cars or counting black-and-white cows, but after an hour or more they were too bored to play anything.

"I'm going to sleep," said Etta and sprawled out on the seat. Paul pinched her legs when they came over to his side. This was half a fight and half a game, and it gradually got more and more noisy.

Mr. Milford said something to his wife and she turned around. "Stop it!" she said. "Your father can't concentrate on the road. You don't want to have an accident, do you?"

They both sat very still for two or three minutes. Then

Etta began to edge her leg over onto Paul's half of the seat. It invaded his territory inch by inch. Paul pretended not to notice. He even shrank more into his own corner and looked out of the window.

Etta watched her mother and edged farther and farther until she had three quarters of the seat. She was still smiling slightly to herself at her victory when Paul pounced on her leg and squeezed the muscle with both hands as hard as he could. Etta howled, more with surprise than pain, and shot back to her own side, lashing out at Paul with her fist. It caught him, more or less by accident, under the ear and he banged his head against the window.

At the same moment Mrs. Milford swung around and brought her hand down in a resounding smack on Etta's bare knee. Etta howled in earnest and hugged the knee to her. "It's not fair," she sobbed. "Why didn't you smack him? It was just as much his fault."

Mrs. Milford didn't answer. She had turned back to the front again and was looking at a map.

"You wait!" whispered Etta to Paul.

Paul's head was still buzzing from the bang on the window. He kept his head turned away so that she shouldn't see the tears that had squeezed themselves out, and pretended to be looking at the trees and fields. After that neither of them spoke until, half an hour later, Mr. Milford pulled the car and trailer onto an open patch of grass at the side of the road.

For the next few minutes everyone was busy winding down the steps of the trailer, getting out the camp chairs, turning on the gas.

"Lunch in half an hour," said Mrs. Milford. "You two go off for a walk somewhere. Have a race up that hill or something. After sitting still so long, you need to get the itches out of your legs."

"How will we know when the half hour's up?" asked Etta. She was still sulking a little, so her voice was stiff and crackly.

"I'll give a good hoot on the horn," said Mr. Milford.

Etta started at once to run up the slope and Paul, after a few seconds of doubt, began to follow her. There was a fence, and as Etta was climbing it she saw Paul coming along. When she was over she waited until he was near enough for her not to have to shout.

"Do you have to go everywhere I go?" she said.

Paul turned away immediately. He pretended he had seen something in the grass. He bent down to look more carefully and then started walking slowly off in a different direction, staring at the ground all the time. Etta watched him for a few seconds, then started to walk up the hill, stretching her long thin legs and swinging her long thin arms.

Paul looked up sideways and saw her go. "You look like a daddy longlegs!" he shouted after her.

Etta went on as if she hadn't heard.

Back in the trailer Mr. and Mrs. Milford saw from the window the two children going their separate ways. "They're not exactly hitting it off at the moment," said Mr. Milford.

"Etta's so used to having everything her own way," said Mrs. Milford. "She's spoiled, that's her trouble."

"I wonder if it'll work," said Mr. Milford. "If only we'd adopted a child when Etta was a baby. It would have been much easier."

"But we didn't. No use crying over lost chances. But

they'll settle down all right, given time. They're bound to quarrel now and then. It wouldn't be natural if they didn't."

"Perhaps you're right," said Mr. Milford.

Paul went back to the trailer before the half hour was up. He didn't go inside but sat down on the grass and sorted out the treasures he had found in the grass. When he first started looking down he had been pretending, but soon he had started to find odd things, and now he had quite a collection. He put them in a row to admire them.

First there was a bright-orange cartridge case, an empty one from a shotgun, then a whole lot of small bleached bones, very fine and delicate, like pieces of ivory. One of them, the one he liked best, was the shoulder blade of a mouse. The flat part was as thin as a cigarette paper. Then there were three or four odd-shaped pebbles of different colors, and finally, the prize of the whole collection, a young slowworm. This was about seven or eight inches long, black along its back but fading off to a rich copper color underneath, and with two beautiful golden stripes that ran down either side of its body. Paul handled it very carefully, remembering reading somewhere that the tails were very fragile.

Mr. Milford came out a few minutes later to hoot the car horn to say that lunch was ready.

"You're back already," he said. "What have you got there?"

Paul showed him his things one at a time, ending up with the slowworm.

"Say, isn't he a beauty?" Mr. Milford took the slowworm and let it wind in and out of his fingers.

"Can I keep it for a pet?"

"If you want to."

"What should I feed it?"

"I forget. But there's a book in the car that might tell you."

He went over to the car, and after giving a long hoot came back with a fat nature book in his hands. He flipped the pages.

"Ah, here it is. Doesn't say very much. I guess you know it's a lizard and not a snake. Now, this is the part. *Feeds mainly on worms and slugs, particularly the small white kind.* That's it, then."

"Where will I find them?"

"Among the grass roots, probably. But let's have lunch first, eh?"

Paul put the slowworm gently into his jacket pocket and went into the trailer. He was careful when he sat down not to crush that particular pocket. They started eating and five minutes later Etta had still not come.

"I'll give her another hoot," said Mr. Milford, and did so.

Another five minutes passed and still she didn't come.

"She's probably sulking," said Mrs. Milford.

"She might have been too far away to hear. Or perhaps the wind is carrying the sound in the wrong direction," said Mr. Milford. He got out of the trailer and looked around.

Paul stood by him for a moment looking up at the empty hillside. "I made her cross because I kept on following her," he said.

Mr. Milford looked at him, frowning a little because he didn't understand what Paul was talking about.

"I'll go and get her," Paul added. "I don't think she's gone very far."

Mr. Milford was doubtful. "It won't help much if you get lost too."

"I won't get lost," said Paul with confidence.

"Well . . . there's no desperate hurry, All right, then. We'll do the dishes and get ready to move on and then wait for you."

Paul grinned and hurried off. He was quite sure in his own mind that Etta was just being difficult. She was probably sitting under a bush sulking, just out of sight over the hill. He'd soon bring her back.

9 . Lost and Found

When Etta had left Paul at the fence and gone striding up toward the top of the hill, she had been in no mood to look around her or notice the way she was going. Even at the best of times she was never very observant, but now, miserable and furious at the same time, screwed up inside, hot, stretched, ready to burst, she stamped on her way with only the vaguest notion of what was around her.

She reached the first brow of the hill, but turned aside at the top, ran down a slope, up another, turned the corner of a small wood and then, in a place where the sun was warm and there was no wind, she sat down on a tree stump, put her chin in her hands, and gave in to the misery of feeling that she was not wanted.

Hot tears ran down her cheeks for a while. She didn't try sensibly to ask herself why she was in such a state, she just let her misery grow and grow on its own accord. In the end she flung herself face downward on the short turf and moaned and wept into the grass roots. When she had worn herself out she fell asleep.

When she awoke she had no idea of how much time had passed. The sun had gone behind a thick cloud and it seemed very late. She was hungry. She could hardly remember now what had made her so miserable, but she gloated a little at the idea of her mother and father and Paul being worried about her.

"It'd be a good idea never to go back," she told herself. "Then they'd be sorry. And serve them right."

She saw a picture of them getting sadly into the car and driving off. She saw them traveling on, their faces set with misery, not speaking. Every now and again her mother would turn and stare sadly at the empty place on the back seat. Then she saw them at home, saw Paul packing up his things and leaving without a word, saw her parents sitting on either side of the fireplace, not reading, not speaking, not even looking at television.

Suddenly the vision vanished. "That's silly," she said. "They must be looking for me. They wouldn't just go!"

She jumped to her feet and looked around to see which way she had come. She couldn't remember. She was in a sort of hollow surrounded by three hills, all more or less alike. She remembered she had come over a hill but couldn't decide which of the three it had been. She had to choose by tapping it out with her own private rhyme.

> *Henrietta Milford*
> *One, two, three,*
> *Doesn't like tomatoes*
> *Or eggs for her tea.*
> *When it comes to teatime*
> *They all shout,*
> *Henrietta Milford,*
> *YOU—WALK—OUT!*

When she had finally chosen a hill, she didn't like its looks at all. It seemed the wrong shape for a start. But as she had chosen it, she had to try that one first, so off she went.

By the time she reached the top, she was feeling quite weary. The wind seemed to be blowing much harder than it had before, and with the sun quenched by the cloud, it seemed suddenly to be cold. Etta stood on the windy hilltop and looked slowly around in a complete circle. There was no road, no red car, no homely sheltering trailer. Only miles and miles of fields and woods with, a very long way off, a cluster of houses that must have been a village.

Oh, well, she thought. Try another one.

This time she didn't tap it out but examined the two remaining hills very carefully. One of them had a smooth, almost flat top and the other had a sort of blister or bump on it. As if the hill had a pimple, she thought. Well, I'm sure it wasn't that one or I'd have noticed it.

So she trotted down her hill and started slowly up the second. Now that she was tired this took longer, and she had to rest a few times before she reached the top. Again there was no road to be seen. Just a very long, smooth slope down and, very small in the distance, a fence.

There was a fence, she thought, because that was where she told Paul to stop following her. It must be it. Perhaps the car and the trailer were around the corner of those trees. She never looked back to see if they were in sight. And the road might be around the corner too.

Having convinced herself it was the right direction at last, she started off down the slope, trotting at first but then slowing to a walk as she got wearier. It was an awful long way, that was certain.

When she was halfway to the fence she began to have doubts again. Surely it couldn't have been as far as this? She seemed to have walked miles. If the hill had been that far off, she would never have climbed it in the first place. She turned around to look back at the hill and it seemed to be the wrong shape. The other two were out of sight. She felt like crying again.

For a few minutes she stood where she was, trying to make up her mind whether to go on or to go back and try the third hill. Then her eye caught a glimpse of red through the screen of trees to the left of the fence. It was only a tiny patch but just enough to make her decide to go on. It just had to be the car.

At last she reached the fence and climbed it. There was still no road to be seen, but the red through the trees was there about a hundred yards away to the left. She broke

into an exhausted run toward the trees. Gasping for breath and sobbing, she went around the corner and found herself staring at a bright-red farm tractor. She threw herself down on the ground again and stared up with tear-filled eyes at the gray stupid sky.

A few minutes later, however, she sat up and rubbed her eyes fiercely. "Henrietta Milford," she said sternly, "you're being a silly crybaby. You've been lost before, hundreds of times. And anyway, it just serves you right, stamping off in such a temper. Now just get yourself up and do something sensible."

Following her own instructions she stood up, brushed the grass seeds off her dress, and looked around. The hill she had just come down seemed so far away that for a moment she could not bear the thought of retracing her footsteps. She turned slowly. She was on the edge of a field of stubble. The line of trees led down to a gate at the corner of the field and on the other side of the gate there was a road. But it was only a small road, much smaller than the one they had been traveling on just before they stopped for lunch.

It was no use trying to go on; she just had to turn back and climb that horrid hill again. She swung around and began to plod miserably up the long slope. She knew that any moment now she would start crying. If there was one thing that really frightened her, it was the idea of getting lost.

"Etta! Etta!"

She stopped immediately and looked eagerly up the slope. The hill was blurred with rainbow colors because she was looking through tears. She wiped her eyes quickly and looked again.

"Etta! Etta!"

It was Paul's voice; she was quite sure of that. But the hillside ahead was still quite empty.

"Etta! This way! Turn around!"

It was like a voice out of the clouds. She turned slowly around like a weathercock facing a new wind and there, not very far away, was the figure of Paul waving with both arms and running toward her. She ran to meet him.

They stopped a few feet apart, panting. Neither of them seemed quite sure what to say.

Paul said, "They're ready to go now. I said I'd come and tell you."

They walked side by side.

"Are they cross?" Etta said.

"No, I don't think so."

Paul looked at Etta out of the corner of his eye and he thought she still looked a little solemn. "Sorry I kept on following you," he said.

"I don't mind really."

They went on until they could see the trailer and car below them. Mr. Milford saw them and waved.

"Look what I found," Paul said. He took the slowworm out of his pocket and showed it to her. "You can have it if you like."

Etta took it, enjoying the hard, leathery feel of it in her hands. Then she said, "I'd rather let it go."

Paul hesitated, but only for a moment. "Go on then," he said.

He felt a pang of loss as he watched the slowworm disappear in the matted grass. There was a hoot from the waiting car, so they both started off again.

"Thanks for coming to find me," said Etta when they were almost there.

"It's all right," he said.

10 . Many Changes

At the end of vacation Mr. Milford took Paul back to the Home. Mr. Truman was just coming out of his office as they drove up. After greeting them he said to Paul, "Don't run away, Paul. I want to chat with you in a minute."

He went into his office with Mr. Milford and Paul sat on the grass at the side of the drive wondering what they were saying to each other. He wondered if Mr. Milford was complaining about him. He and Etta had quarreled rather a lot in the past two weeks. It was mostly her fault, but Mr. Milford would be on her side, naturally.

He could hear their voices bumbling away inside the office, but he couldn't hear the actual words. They seemed to be laughing quite a lot. With grown-ups you couldn't tell whether that was a good sign or not. They seemed to laugh at anything. One thing he was pretty sure about— the Milfords wouldn't ask him to stay with them again. "I don't care," he thought to himself.

He knew that wasn't quite true. He liked them really. Even Etta was all right, only she drove him mad sometimes, and then he did silly things.

The door of the office opened and Mr. Truman and Mr. Milford came out. Paul saw they both looked cheerful. Mr. Milford patted him on the head as he passed on his way to the car.

"Cheerio, Paul. See you soon!" he said.

Paul stood up. "Good-bye Mr. Milford," he said. As he watched the car drive away he felt depressed.

"Well," said Mr. Truman. "Mr. Milford's been telling me

about your trip. Sounds as if you had a lot of fun."

Paul looked suspiciously at Mr. Truman to see if he could tell from his expression whether he was serious or having a joke. He seemed serious. "It was all right," he said cautiously.

"Sounded better than all right to me," said Mr. Truman.

"They don't like me very much," Paul said.

"I'm sure you're wrong. Mr. Milford was saying how nice it was to have a boy in the family."

"Oh, he's all right," Paul said. "I like him. It's the other two. And Mrs. Milford was always telling me off about something or other."

"Always?"

"She does it an awful lot," Paul complained.

"About what?"

"About nothing. About eating properly and saying please and thank you, and she keeps on saying I'm teasing Etta when it's mostly her fault, oh, and everything. . . ."

"Most mothers are like that," said Mr. Truman with a laugh. "That's not telling off. That's teaching you how to behave properly. I'm sure she does it to Etta as well."

"She does it to everyone," said Paul. "She even tells Mr. Milford not to drop ashes on the rug, and once she made him put his tie on when we were going to the movies—in the dark, where no one could see him!"

"Well, there you are. So it wasn't specially you, was it?"

"I suppose not."

There was a pause and Mr. Truman muttered something about supposing it would sort itself out.

"Can I go up to the house now?" Paul asked.

"Yes, of course. That was what I wanted to talk about really. I'll come along with you."

Paul took his suitcase and they walked side by side

through the woods toward the house. Paul wanted to run, but he had to be polite and keep up with Mr. Truman, who seemed in no hurry but walked very slowly, looking at the ground as if thinking. After a few steps he cleared his throat.

"We've had a few changes while you've been away," he said at last. "I thought I'd better warn you."

Paul waited. From the way Mr. Truman was behaving he guessed it was something he wouldn't like.

"Rosine's gone," said Mr. Truman. "She was only here for a year in any case, getting experience and learning the language, you see."

There was another pause and they went a few more steps.

"And Jock's gone too, but that's good news really."

"Why is it good news? I liked Jock."

"We all did. What happened was his mother got married again and she's got a nice house and has settled down again and she wanted to have her children back."

Paul thought about this. "That's a lot of changes all right."

"I haven't quite finished. Sadi's mother has finished her training. She decided to go back to Pakistan, and of course Sadi went with her."

Paul stopped and let his suitcase fall to the ground. "That means everyone's gone!" he exclaimed. "It'll all be different now." He felt his eyes prickling and knew that in a minute he wouldn't be able to stop himself from crying.

Mr. Truman picked up his suitcase and put his other hand on Paul's shoulder. "I knew it would be a bit of a shock," he said. "I'm afraid you have to get used to changes in a place like this. It's rather like a railway station—people coming and going all the time. I'm sorry it all happened while you were away. Makes it harder to take. Sadi left you a note and I have their address, so you can write to her if you want to."

He handed Paul a crumpled envelope which Paul pushed into his pocket. They had reached the front door of the house now, but Paul was no longer in a hurry to go in; he had a dreadful empty feeling. "I wish I didn't have to come back," he said, feeling the tears start.

"I know how you feel," said Mr. Truman, and then thought to himself that he didn't really know. "Oh, dear," he sighed, and then said in his more cheerful voice, "Well, anyway, you'd better come in and meet your new house-mother. Her name is Mrs. Wood." He opened the front door. "There she is, in the kitchen," he added.

"But she's old!" said Paul.

"Er . . . yes . . . well, come on!"

For the next two days Paul wandered around like someone lost. If it had only been two weeks later he would have had school to keep him busy, but it was still the summer vacation, and there seemed nothing whatever to do. There were two new children in the house, but he didn't like either of them and kept well out of their way. He went up to the swimming pool once or twice, but there was no fun in swimming anymore. He and Sadi had learned to swim at the same time and had always gone together. There didn't seem to be any sense in swimming by himself.

Even the tree-walk had lost its attraction. He only went on it when Evelyn asked him to help her, and she must have felt that his heart wasn't in it for she soon gave up asking him. He kept the note from Sadi in his pocket. She had only written what he knew already—that she had gone to Pakistan with her mother and that she wouldn't ever be coming back to England. The last part of the letter was about all the relations she was going to meet again—her father and two brothers, her grandmother and grandfather, her cousins and uncles and so on. She ended with, "I am very happy and excited to think I shall so soon be seeing them all again." And then she signed her name and that was all. Nothing about being sorry to leave. Nothing at all like that. Paul carried the letter around with him, but he did not write an answer to it, even though she had given the address in Pakistan. There didn't seem any point.

Mr. Truman guessed how Paul was feeling and tried to find jobs to keep him busy. Thursday was stores day, and Paul was kept very busy the whole day helping to sort out the right amounts of tea, sugar, flour, jam, cans of fruit, and beans and spaghetti and other groceries for each of the houses.

On Friday Mr. Truman took Paul shopping into Canterbury to get odd things like nails and screws, paint for the bathroom wall where the two new children had scratched and scribbled and drawn pictures, new blades for the lawn mower, some typing paper for the office, and half a dozen other odds and ends that the housemothers had asked him about during the week. Paul enjoyed the trip. Canterbury was so bright and colorful and busy, and it made a change from the peace and quiet of Magsted.

When all the shopping had been done, Mr. Truman said, "Let's put all these in the back of the car and then go off for ice cream or a soda or something, shall we?"

Paul nodded. "Can we go to that place with all the pigeons?" he asked.

"I think they've been having a purge on pigeons lately," said Mr. Truman. "But we could go and see."

"What do you mean, a purge on them?"

"Well, they've been trying to get rid of them. There were so many that it was doing damage to the cathedral."

The place that Paul meant was a café on the flat roof over a shop in the Longmarket. There was an indoor part and an outdoor part with sunshades and bright plastic-seated chairs. You could look down on all the busy traffic and shoppers, and the last time Paul had been there he had fed the pigeons that flew down from the roofs and gutters all around. They were so tame they would sit on your wrist and eat out of your hand.

But this time there were hardly any pigeons to be seen, and there was a large sign fixed to the rails that said "Please do not feed the pigeons."

"Pigeons can't read," said Paul, "so how do they know? They wouldn't all fly away just because someone told them to."

Mr. Truman pointed up to the edge of the nearest roof. "Look at that roof," he said. "There used to be about a hundred sitting in a hungry row along there."

"They've put black putty stuff all along the edge," said Paul.

"That's right. The pigeons don't like landing on that because their feet sink in. So in the end they fly away somewhere else."

"Etta wouldn't like that," Paul said. "She'd do her act about people being cruel and all that. She's nuts about animals. Do you know she wouldn't even let me kill a wasp."

Mr. Truman laughed, and then he said, "I had a letter from the Milfords today."

"Did they say anything about me?"

"It was all about you, as a matter of fact."

Paul had a nasty cold feeling. Having made up his mind that he hadn't behaved very nicely during his fortnight of vacationing with the Milfords, he had tried not to think about them. He wished he hadn't said anything about Etta. Then Mr. Truman wouldn't have remembered about the letter.

"Shall I tell you about it?" asked Mr. Truman.

Paul fiddled with his empty soda bottle. He tried to see if he could join both the straws together to make one very long one. "All right," he said.

"Aren't you interested?"

"Depends what they said."

"They want you to go and live with them."

"For this weekend?"

"For ever," said Mr. Truman.

It was like having a live bomb put in your lap. Paul stared at Mr. Truman in a daze. "You must be joking," he said.

"No, I'm quite serious. And so are they. But you don't have to make up your mind all in one jump. I'll explain how it works, shall I?"

Paul sucked in his cheeks to try to find some moisture for his throat, which had suddenly gone dry and crackly. He nodded.

"Well, to start off, there'd be a trial period. You'd stay with them for a few months and they would be what we call foster parents."

"I had foster parents in Maidstone," said Paul. "They were horrible."

"Yes, I know. Well, we'd hope this would be different. Still, the point is if you were unhappy or for some reason you couldn't get along with them you'd only have to tell us and you could come back."

"Back to Magsted?"

"I guess so."

"You said for ever."

"If it worked out well and you were happy with them, then after a few months they might apply to adopt you."

"What's the difference?"

"That's the forever bit. It makes them your real parents and it makes you a proper part of the family."

"Then I'd have my own family—like Sadi. Uncle and cousins and all the rest of it?"

"That's right."

Paul thought about it for a short while. "What do I have to say?" he asked at last.

"You don't have to say anything right away. But if you like the idea, I could write back and tell them to go ahead with the plans."

"How soon would I go there?"

Mr. Truman shrugged his shoulders. "Everything takes time, of course. A couple of weeks, maybe."

"All right," Paul said. "I'll go."

As soon as he said it he felt wonderfully free. It was as if he had been tied up in yards and yards of rope, around his ribs and legs and arms and even his head, and all at once someone had cut the knots and he was able to breathe and move easily again. He took a very deep breath, stretching up in his chair and feeling his ribs with his fingers.

"Are you all right?" asked Mr. Truman. "Do you want anything?"

"I want to shout," said Paul.

Mr. Truman waved a hand. "Don't mind me," he said. "Go right ahead!"

Paul let out the beginnings of a shout, but the moment people's heads swiveled sharply around to look at him, the rest of it died in his throat. He let his breath out carefully.

11 . Paul Makes a New Start

The last two weeks of the vacation trickled by so slowly that Etta could not believe that anything was being done. "Surely," she exclaimed to her father, "they can't take all this time to write a few letters?"

"I guess there are a lot of official things to be done," said Mr. Milford. "And I suppose everything has to be checked to see if it's right."

The Milfords were visited again by Miss Mallim, and this time she really did go upstairs and look at the bedrooms, especially at the spare room which was to be Paul's own room when he came. When Etta asked her when Paul would be coming she didn't seem very sure.

"Are you looking forward to it a lot?" she asked.

"Well, of course. Wouldn't you be?"

Miss Mallim smiled. "I don't know," she said. "I had lots of brothers and sisters of my own. I don't really know what it's like to be just one."

"It's horrid," said Etta immediately.

"All the time?" asked Miss Mallim with a smile.

"Not all the time, I suppose."

Miss Mallim smiled in a knowing sort of way but didn't say any more. Etta was puzzled by her and when she had gone asked her mother.

Mrs. Milford also smiled in the same knowing way. "I guess she thought to herself that you're rather a spoiled little girl and you might find it hard to share everything from now on."

"Well, we won't have to share *everything* completely,"

said Etta. "We won't have half an egg for breakfast or half an ice-cream cone, or half a bed. You'll have to buy twice as much, won't you?"

"Miss Mallim was probably not thinking of things you buy."

"What else is there?"

"There's things you do, for instance. Suppose you want to watch one television program and Paul wants another. What happens then?"

"We have the one I want, because I'm older," said Etta immediately.

"But that's not sharing."

"Well then, we have what I want one day and what Paul wants the next."

"Think how cross you were about that tennis program."

"Think how cross Paul gets sometimes."

"Exactly," said Mrs. Milford. "You both like having your own way. And then you'll have to share us, won't you? Have you thought of that?"

"I won't mind that," said Etta. "Perhaps when there's two of us you won't be after me so much."

"We'll see, won't we?" said her mother.

Then, two days before Etta was due to go back to school again, they got a letter to say everything had been fixed and Mr. Milford could bring Paul from Magsted as soon as he liked.

"Go down there now!" said Etta. "I'll come with you."

"Now, in the middle of breakfast?"

"You can finish your breakfast if you like."

"I've got to go to work," said Mr. Milford. "I'll phone Mr. Truman from the office, though, and arrange something."

"Arrange to get Paul tonight."

"I'll see what Mr. Truman says."

"Why are you being so beastly?" demanded Etta.

"Because I'm beastly by nature," said Mr. Milford.

"You are too."

Mrs. Milford intervened and told Etta off for having such a cross face and Etta got up and stamped away from the table in a temper.

Mrs. Milford sighed. "It's not going to be easy," she said.

Later in the day Mr. Milford phoned from the office to tell them that Mr. Truman had offered to bring Paul up himself the next day. By this time Etta had got over her crossness.

"I'm going to smother the house with signs saying 'Welcome Paul,'" she said.

"And I'll cook his favorite dinner," said Mrs. Milford.

"Sausages and potato chips and jelly roll."

"No," said her mother, "that's your favorite. He likes macaroni and cheese and bananas and custard."

Etta made a face. "Bananas—ugh!" she said.

"At the moment," said Mrs. Milford, "we're thinking of Paul, aren't we?"

"Yes, but . . ." Etta began, but then she saw the look in her mother's eyes and stopped. "Oh, all right," she grumbled. "I suppose so."

By the time Paul arrived the following day, the house really was smothered in welcome signs. Etta had had plenty of time to make them. She had started off with very elaborate ones with pictures of Paul arriving with his suitcases and all the Milfords standing on the step to greet him. There was one on the wall over the table with a picture of all four sitting down to a huge meal big enough for at least a dozen people. There was a simply splendid arrangement in his bedroom with letters so big that the sign covered the whole of one wall. Then she ran out of ideas and made half a dozen with just the word "Welcome" and put these in all sorts of unexpected places. And finally she had the idea of hanging a clothes line outside the house from one bedroom window to another and pegging sheets of paper on the line. Each piece of paper had one letter on it and the whole message read "Paul arrives today hurray hurray hurray."

Paul got out of Mr. Truman's car and saw this sign first. He stood and read it slowly. Mr. Truman got his bag out of the back and then looked up. "Red-carpet treatment," he said.

Paul looked puzzled but didn't say anything more just then. They went in. There was a feverish air about the house and Paul felt it right away. Mrs. Milford didn't look any different, but her voice had a strained sound and there were little lines around her eyes as if she were worried about something. After she had greeted them both she told Paul to go and find Etta. "She's in such a state I sent her out to clean her rabbit hutch," Mrs. Milford said

to Mr. Truman. "Go and find her, Paul. You know where to go, don't you?"

Paul looked at Mr. Truman.

"I'll give you a shout before I leave."

"All right," Paul said and went off.

As soon as Etta saw him she started talking and she went on getting quicker and quicker so that Paul couldn't get a word in. Even when she asked him questions she didn't wait for the answers. She told him about the letter that had come and what she had said to her father and what he had answered. She told him about the special lunch Mrs. Milford had prepared for him and about the flowers in his room and about how she had spent the whole morning making welcome signs.

"I've only seen one," Paul said, managing to interrupt her. "That was the one out front. Mrs. Milford sent me right out here, so I didn't have time to see any more."

"Did you like it?" said Etta. "You can't call her Mrs. Milford anymore, you'll have to say Mum like I do."

"I don't see why. She isn't my mother really."

"She will be when you're properly adopted."

"Suppose I don't want to be?" Paul didn't mean to say this; it just came out. Perhaps he didn't like being taken for granted. "Mr. Truman said it all depended on how I felt later."

"Of course you will be," cried Etta, jumping to her feet and getting very red in the face. "You can't spoil it now, after all the trouble it's been!"

"I can do what I like," said Paul. "And I thought your sign out front was soppy. Like a lot of old laundry on a line. And anyway, why does it say 'Hurry, hurry, hurry'?"

"You didn't even read it right," cried Etta, on the brink

of tears. "It says 'Hurray,' and I think you're the beastliest person I've ever met."

She ran off, leaving him standing by the rabbit hutch, and spent the next five minutes rushing round the house collecting all her signs and tearing them up. Her mother, who had just gone out to the kitchen to make Mr. Truman some coffee, saw her putting them all in the garbage pail and called to her from the kitchen window.

"I'm just throwing away a lot of soppy old rubbish," said Etta, keeping her head turned away from her mother.

"They look like your famous welcome signs to me."

"What if they are? Paul thinks they're soppy."

"I'm sure he doesn't. Oh, dear, I knew you were getting too excited. I suppose you two started right off with a quarrel."

"I didn't start it," she snapped and, slamming the garbage-pail lid down, she went into the house and stamped her way upstairs to her bedroom.

About ten minutes passed while she sulked on the bed and then her mood began to disappear. She crept out and stood at the top of the stairs listening. She could hear Mr. Truman's voice from the living room, and her mother's and also that of Paul joining in. She felt left out in the cold. She crept slowly down the stairs and stood for a while by the living-room door trying to summon up enough courage to go in, but somehow she couldn't persuade her hand to reach out and turn the knob. In the end she wandered through the house and out through the French windows again. Perhaps someone would call her. She sat down on the step waiting, but no one did.

Bored with doing nothing she got up and thought she would go around to the front to see if Mr. Truman's car was still outside in the road. But before she got there she had to pass the rabbit hutch and the first thing she noticed was that the door was wide open and the hutch empty.

"But I latched it! I remember latching it," she thought. Then she remembered leaving Paul standing just there in front of the hutch. He must have opened the door to pay her back.

In desperation she searched the garden. It wasn't very big, and there weren't many places Gretel could hide. The only danger was that she could squeeze through one part of the back fence and get out onto the slopes above the sea. She had done it once before and a huge German shepherd had chased her around the bushes and finally caught her in its huge mouth. Luckily the dog's owner had been near and shouted at the dog just in time. Gretel had been very frightened and her fur had been wet and plastered down with the dog's saliva but otherwise she

hadn't been harmed. Now, with no one to look after her, it might be different.

Etta searched the garden once again, looking in every place big enough for the rabbit to hide in, but found nothing. Then she opened the gate and ran out through the back lane onto the slopes. There were two dogs some way off. One of them was a fox terrier, and fox terriers were the very worst sort of dog so far as rabbits were concerned. Etta walked around the slopes calling and peering under the low bushes. She didn't dare leave until the dogs had gone.

As soon as they were put on their leads and taken off by their owners, Etta ran back into the house. She burst straight into the living room where her mother, Mr. Truman, and Paul were sitting around talking.

"Did you let Gretel out of her hutch?" she demanded angrily.

Paul made a comical sort of face and stared up at the ceiling as if trying to remember. "I just might have," he said in a drawling voice.

"Don't show off," said Etta. "You either did or you didn't."

Mrs. Milford and Mr. Truman looked from one to the other but didn't interfere.

"I can't find her anywhere in the garden," said Etta. "If a dog gets her out on the slopes . . ."

Paul stood up. "I don't suppose she's gone far," he said. "I'll come and help you find her."

Etta couldn't think of anything really cutting to say to that, so she made a snorting noise and stamped out. Paul followed, smiling knowingly to himself and obviously enjoying some private joke.

When they reached the hutch Etta pointed at the door

still hanging open. "See!" she said accusingly. "I always shut it and latch it. You opened it, didn't you?"

Paul still smiled and then said, in a preaching sort of voice, "It's cruel to keep wild animals shut up."

"Gretel's not wild. And anyway it's not the same. . . ."

At the back of her mind Etta realized the justice of this, but she was so worried about what might have happened to Gretel that she didn't let herself listen. She started going around the garden for the third time.

"Did you think of looking under here?" asked Paul.

She turned and saw that he was standing by the grass catcher of the lawn mower. Her father always turned it over so that rain water didn't get in and make it rusty. Paul was tapping on the green-painted metal with his fingers and there was something about the look on his face that made Etta suspicious. She went slowly across the lawn. "How could she get under there?" she said.

Paul shrugged his shoulders but said nothing.

Etta lifted the grass catcher slowly. Gretel hopped out and after a brief look around shook her ears and started to eat grass.

"You pig!" said Etta violently. "You put her under there on purpose, didn't you? I'm never going to talk to you again."

Out in the road by the car, Mr. Truman was saying good-bye to Mrs. Milford. "Don't take it too seriously," he was saying. "You're bound to have a little teething trouble to begin with. Paul's not an easy boy. He likes to have his own way. It may take some time for him to get used to the idea of giving in to others now and then."

"Etta's the same, I'm afraid," said Mrs. Milford.

"Two of a kind, eh?" Mr. Truman said with a laugh.

12 . Two of a Kind

It didn't make it any easier for Paul that the day after he went to live with the Milfords he had to start at a new school. His first feelings about it were that it was a very unfriendly place full of unfriendly people. Mrs. Milford went with him on this first day and had a long talk with the principal. Etta, however, who had still not forgiven him for the affair of the rabbit, would have nothing to do with him in the playground. He saw her once or twice during the day. She was with a group of her friends, and once, when they all turned and stared at him, he felt sure she had just been telling them about how he had hidden Gretel under the grass catcher.

The children in his class didn't seem eager to be friends with him and the teacher had a dreadful cold and was snappy with everyone. The only boy who did offer to be friendly was a big, overgrown fellow from the top class, years older than Paul, who didn't have any friends of his own age and was also somewhat dumb. Paul didn't mind this at first. It was a relief to have someone to play with, although he soon found out why this boy didn't have any friends. The only thing he really enjoyed was twisting people's arms. When Paul found this out he tried to keep out of the boy's way, and he had a thoroughly miserable time of it until the playground teacher happened to notice what was going on and sent the big boy about his business.

The first day dragged by like a nightmare made of rub-

101

ber. At the end of it Paul emerged from the school gates and took a deep breath with the feeling that for the first time for ages he didn't have to be on his guard. The school was only about half a mile from the Milfords' house, and as he didn't expect Etta to wait for him, he started to walk back.

When he got to the house, he wasn't sure whether to knock or simply walk in. He hesitated a moment and then thought, "Well, I do live here now," and opened the door.

"Is that you, Etta?" called Mrs. Milford from the kitchen.

"No, it's me."

"Isn't Etta with you?"

"No."

"I told her to wait. I wonder if . . . oh, never mind." Mrs. Milford came into the passage and smiled at him. "You poor lamb," she said. "You look absolutely worn out. Was it dreadful?"

"It was all right," said Paul, who didn't want to think about it anymore.

"Have a glass of cold milk."

Paul waited while she got the milk from the refrigerator. Then he said, "Do you mind if I take it upstairs to my room? I think I'd like a little rest."

"Good idea. I'll call you when it's time to eat."

Paul sat on his bed and drank the cool milk. It was quiet and peaceful in his room. He thought that having a bedroom all to himself was the best thing that had ever happened to him. He lay back on the bed and watched the curtain moving in the soft breeze that blew through the open window. His arm ached from where that boy had kept twisting it, and his head ached from all the bustle and worry of school. He felt vaguely lost and miserable.

He thought about Sadi for a few minutes, but that was no use because she had gone. Then he thought about Jock going back to his mother, and about the father who never came to see him. Nobody ever used those paints his father had sent. Or perhaps they had by now, once they'd forgotten about Jock and his birthday. He wondered if they had forgotten about him, back at the Home. Mr. Truman wouldn't forget, but the others kept changing. There wouldn't be anybody to remember after a while. In the whole world there wasn't a single person who cared where he was. The Milfords were all right, but they didn't really know him. And Etta hated him.

He climbed off the bed and got his suitcase from underneath it. There was a wallet in it, a very old and battered wallet, with "Hugh Aintree" printed on the front in faint gold letters. It was the only thing he had from his father.

There wasn't anything in the wallet; he never used it for anything. In fact, he didn't know why he kept it. His father was probably dead anyway. No one had ever heard from him, they said.

Paul threw the wallet back in the suitcase and kicked it under the bed. He went over and stood by the window, which faced out over the back of the garden and miles and miles of dirty-green sea. He could just see one of the forts in the far distance standing up out of the water like an oil rig. He wondered what it would be like to live right out there, miles from anyone. They said there had once been pirate radio stations there. He wondered if he was clever enough to be a disk jockey. The next time someone asked what he was going to be when he was grown up, that's what he'd say. "I'm going to be a disk jockey on a pirate radio."

His head was aching dreadfully. He thought of going down and asking Mrs. Milford for an aspirin or something. He decided to leave it until dinner time. He stretched out on the bed again and then, feeling slightly chilly, he took his shoes off and pulled a blanket over himself. He closed his eyes.

The door burst open and Etta stood there glaring at him. "You might have waited," she said. "I stood there for hours, until the very last person had gone home."

"I didn't know you were going to wait."

"Of course you knew. You just thought it would be a good trick to play on me. Just being your usual beastly self!"

She slammed the door as she went.

Paul turned his head to the wall and pulled the blanket up to cover himself completely.

Paul stayed in bed for the next two days with a very bad

cold. Etta came up after school to see how he was. She brought his dinner on a tray. She didn't actually say she was sorry for being so cross the day before, but she looked sorry. She put the tray on the bedside table and sat down.

"I told Mrs. Franklin you'd caught her cold," she said. "Mum says teachers oughtn't to be allowed to take their germs to school and spread them all around the class like that."

Paul saw that Etta was trying to be friendly. He didn't feel much like talking but he didn't mind listening. He ate a slice of bread and butter and drank some milk and then lay down again.

"What about the fruit cake?" asked Etta. "Mum thought you liked fruit cake. She bought it especially for you."

"I do, usually," Paul said. "I'm not very hungry just now."

"Can I have it?"

"I don't care."

Etta ate the fruit cake and told him about everything that had happened at school that day. Paul didn't know all the people she was talking about and didn't pay a lot of attention, but the sound of her voice was very pleasant and as he had been alone most of the day he was quite pleased to have company. She went downstairs when it was time for her favorite television program, though.

On the third day Paul felt completely recovered. Mrs. Milford said he could get up if he liked but she wasn't going to let him go to school. "Not after being in bed two days," she said. "You've got to get used to being around. Anyway, it's Friday. Monday will be soon enough."

Paul didn't object. He wasn't at all eager to go to school after his first day's experience. He spent most of the morning on the beach and rather enjoyed himself. There was a stray dog down there that kept bringing him pieces of wood to throw and even when he hurled them as far out to sea as he could, the dog plunged into the water and swam out to retrieve them.

When he got back to the house, feeling exhausted with his exercise, he found that Miss Mallim had called and was sitting in the living room talking to Mrs. Milford. They both looked very serious, and Paul's first thought was to wonder what he could have done wrong. Miss Mallim put a quick smile on, but Mrs. Milford went on looking thoughtful.

"So, here comes the invalid! Looking remarkably healthy however."

She went on chatting to Paul for a few minutes more, asking him the usual kind of questions that people do, then she stood up to go. Paul heard the voices going off down the passage more or less as a jumble of sound. One sentence came back quite clearly though. "I think he ought to be told."

"Sooner or later, of course. I leave it to you to decide when," said Miss Mallim, and then the door closed.

Paul waited until Mrs. Milford came back and then said, "What ought you to tell me?"

"What makes you so sure we were talking about you?" said Mrs. Milford. She was playing for time, saying anything until she had made up her mind.

"You were, though, weren't you?"

"Well, yes. Among other things. Paul, what do you know about your father?"

"I know his name. He was called Hugh Aintree. It's written on an old wallet."

"How do you know it's his wallet?"

Paul tried to remember how he knew this, but nothing came. "I just think it is, that's all. I don't know why."

"And can't you remember anything about him at all? Nothing your mother ever said? Was he with your mother when she died?"

Paul shook his head. "I don't know. I can't remember anything much. But I don't think he was. I only remember something about other people. There was a fat woman, I think she lived next door, she was there. And a doctor and then the ambulance people, and then they took her away. And then they took me away. I didn't see her again."

"You haven't got a picture of your father?"

"No." Of this Paul was quite sure. He could remember that there had been a picture, of his mother and father together. He could just remember that.

"What did he look like?"

"He was shorter than my mother. Short and fat, like me," Paul said. "And he wore glasses. That's all. Why are you asking me all these questions? Miss Mallim told you something, didn't she?"

Mrs. Milford hesitated again, still not sure how to put it. "Well, yes. She said that they've heard from him. They've had a letter inquiring about you."

"Why doesn't he just come if he wants to know about me?"

"He doesn't know where you are yet."

"But they'll tell him?"

"I guess so, dear."

"And then he'll come?"

"I don't know. I'm sorry, Paul, I just don't know."

Paul thought about it and then said in a flat voice, "It doesn't make much difference, does it? He's never been to see me before. It's like Jock's father really, only mine doesn't even send me birthday presents. He wouldn't know me even if he did come."

"Well, there might be a reason for that," said Mrs. Milford. "In the letter he said something about not being in touch with things for a long time."

"Has he been abroad then?"

"We don't know quite what he means." Mrs. Milford had a worried look when she said this, and suddenly Paul knew what she was thinking. He didn't guess, he suddenly remembered hearing some of the words they were saying when he came into the room. It made sense now. Mental home. That was what Miss Mallim had been saying. "Or even in a mental home."

"What do they put people in mental homes for?" he asked. "Because they're mad, isn't it? You think my father's mad, don't you?"

"No, Paul, no!" she cried. She hadn't meant it to go as far as this. "You mustn't think that."

"It's what you think."

"I don't. I just don't know. There are all sorts of possibilities. He could have been abroad, as you said. . . ."

"Or in prison," said Paul.

Mrs. Milford was silent.

"He'd be a criminal then. That's what you think. You think he's a murderer or something."

Mrs. Milford was crying. "Please, Paul, please! Oh, you poor lamb." She put her arms around him and for the first time since he had come to the house she hugged him closely to her. "It doesn't matter, Paul. It doesn't matter. You've got us now. We'll always look after you. I promise."

Paul put his arm around her neck and squeezed. All

sorts of troubles seemed to disappear. For a few moments he let all his thoughts float off and the warmth come into him. He didn't have to think about it anymore.

But the thoughts that had thinned and vanished began to take solid shape again. He remembered that he was being comforted by someone who thought his father was a murderer. He struggled against her arm, pushed himself clear, and stood alone in the center of the room.

"I don't believe it!" he said. He could hear his own voice shouting in the echoing room. "I don't care what you think; it's not true. It's not true!"

Somehow or other he found his way up to his room and stood with his back to the door. He glared around at the walls and the furniture—his bed, the curtains, everything —hating it all, hating everything and everybody. The curtains swayed out in a graceful curve, like a dancer's shawl.

"Don't do that!" he shouted at them. Then he rushed across and, seizing them with both hands, he tugged with all his strength and ripped them down. They were made of thin netting, fine and white. He jabbed his fingers through and tore until he had ripped them into frayed strips. Then he hurled them out of the window and threw himself face down on the bed.

Much later Mrs. Milford crept upstairs and peeped into Paul's room. He was sleeping just where he had thrown himself, pale and utterly exhausted. She found a blanket and put it carefully over him and then crept away again.

Later still, when Mr. Milford had come home from work, she told him what had happened. They both went upstairs to look at him, but when they opened the door the room was empty. Paul had gone.

13 . "It's All My Fault!"

Mr. Truman came out of his house and scowled at the morning. It wasn't like him to scowl at anything, but today, while still at breakfast, he had had a worrying phone call. When it was finished he slammed the phone down and thumped himself back in his seat at the breakfast table.

"Some people!" he exclaimed.

Mrs. Truman poured her husband a fresh cup of coffee and waited.

"Some people," repeated Mr. Truman, "couldn't give sixpence to a tramp without rubbing him up the wrong way so that he wanted to spit in their eye."

"Drink your coffee."

Mr. Truman gulped it down without even noticing it. "I give up!" he exclaimed.

"Are you going to tell me, or do I have to guess?" asked his wife.

"Paul. Paul Aintree. You remember him?"

"Of course I remember him. He's only been gone a week. What has he been doing now?"

"It's not a matter of what he's been doing, it's what others have been doing to Paul."

"Really!" said his wife. "Getting information out of you is harder than getting sardines out of a can."

"Sorry. I'm all worked up, aren't I? Well, that phone

call was to tell me that Paul Aintree has run away from the Milfords."

"He'll probably end up here," said his wife. "The ones who run away almost always do."

"He shouldn't have *wanted* to run away," said Mr. Truman. "I know he's an awkward boy, but the Lord knows he didn't need much. A little bit of motherly love and affection and a place to call home, that's all. You wouldn't think people would find that hard to give, would you? I thought the Milfords were decent, sensible people. You wouldn't think they'd make a bungle of it like this."

"You don't know it's their fault," said his wife. "You're always so hasty. You mustn't jump to conclusions."

"But he's run away, hasn't he? He's the one that jumped to a conclusion, not me. Oh, well, I suppose you're right. Wait and see. Wait and see." Mr. Truman looked at his egg and bacon and then put his knife and fork down. "Well, I can't face that," he said. "I think I'll go up and see if we can make room in his old house for when he does arrive. At least let him see he's wanted somewhere. Botchers and menders, that's all we are. People make messes of each other's lives and then leave us to dry the children's tears!"

He pushed his chair back, stalked out of the house, and greeted an otherwise beautiful morning with a good hearty scowl. When he had taken a few deep breaths of the summer-scented air that drifted to him through the pine woods, his features relaxed a little. He went across to his office, got a bunch of keys, and came right out again and went striding up the path.

Before he had taken a dozen steps, a movement caught his eye and he stopped. It was against the sun, and he had to close his eyelids almost to slits to see anything. Someone was on the tree-walk, just at the corner where it came nearest to his house.

"Is that you, Paul?" he shouted.

"Yes, Mr. Truman."

"Thought it must be. Have you had any breakfast yet?"

"No."

"Come down and get some then!"

He waited, just where he was, while Paul walked slowly to the next rope ladder, climbed down, very deliberately one rung at a time, and then came through the woods toward him. Mr. Truman noticed how untidy, dirty, and

weary the boy looked, but he did not make any comment. He put one hand out and Paul took it, not looking up.

"Egg and bacon do you?"

Paul nodded. He did not want to cry anymore, so it was best not to try and say too much. He walked back toward Mr. Truman's house.

Half an hour later, after a very good breakfast and a hot wash, Paul tried to tell the Trumans how it all happened. He told it in a very muddled way, putting things in the wrong order and forgetting bits and remembering them later, but by the end they had the whole story. Mr. Truman kept pacing up and down the room, then sitting down, then jumping up again and doing some more pacing.

"It shouldn't have happened," he exclaimed. "People blundering about, putting their great big feet everywhere, saying things they ought not to say, hints, suggestions, doubts, thinking this and that. There was no excuse."

"It's easy to understand how it happened, though," said his wife. Not that she really expected to calm him down —they had been married too long for her to make that mistake—but she still felt she ought to try.

"Understand!" he cried. "Of course it's easy to understand—afterward. Any fool can understand—afterward. Nobody wants to be understood. When you understand someone, you turn them into a thing. It's people we're talking about. People ought to feel, use their instincts . . . I don't know . . . have a little common sense. . . ."

He went spluttering on like this for some minutes. When he paused for breath, Mrs. Truman said quietly, "What are you going to do about it?"

"Do?" Mr. Truman's thin hair seemed to stand on end as he shot out the word. "Clear it up, I suppose. We can't have this boy not knowing about his own father, can we?"

"It's not really your job, dear."

"I can't make a worse mess of it than it's in already," said Mr. Truman. "I'll make a start on that Mallim female and see what she really knows. I'll use the office phone. Don't go away, Paul."

When he had dashed out, Paul felt rather apprehensive. He turned to Mrs. Truman. "Will I get the Milfords into trouble?" he said. "Mrs. Milford's nice, really. She didn't actually say anything. And she cried like anything when I kept asking her questions. She couldn't help it, could she?"

"No, dear, of course not. And no one will get into trouble. Mr. Truman always flies off the handle like that, but once he's had time to settle down he's quite nice and kind and sensible."

"But he called Miss Mallim a female."

Mrs. Truman laughed. "They get along quite well together in fact," she said. "It'll all come right in the end, you'll see."

Paul thought about this for a while and then said, "All the same, I'd rather not go back and live there. Do you think it would matter if I didn't?"

"You won't have to do anything you don't want to do," she said. "Let's wait and see, shall we?"

The Milfords were very quiet over their breakfast. None of them had slept very much, and each one showed it in one way or another. Mr. Milford, who had spent most of the night driving around in his car in the rather misty hope that he might see Paul in the headlights, looked gray and weary. Etta had red eyelids from too much crying. Mrs. Milford looked worst of all, for besides not having slept she also had the nagging thought that she was mostly to blame for what had happened.

"I really think we ought to have told the police," she said. "I'm sure they would have found him by now."

"I told you what Miss Mallim said," said Mr. Milford. "She said they liked to handle it themselves, and anyway, he would almost certainly make for Magsted."

"I just don't like to think of him out all alone in the night. He's only a child. . . ."

The phone rang and Mr. Milford leaped up to answer it. They could hear his voice, but they could not gather from his brief answers what was going on. When he came back he sat down heavily in his chair. "That was Truman from the Home," he said. "He was absolutely furious. Paul's arrived there and told him what happened."

"Thank God for that. Then he's safe," Mrs. Milford said. "I blame myself. If only I'd thought before I spoke . . . but he was so quick . . . and anyway he must have heard what Miss Mallim was saying. . . ."

"It's all my fault," Etta burst out passionately. "I was horrid to him the very first moment he arrived. I don't know what came over me. I couldn't seem to stop it either. It just went on and on."

"I think we all made somewhat of a mess of it," said Mr. Milford. "We expected too much of him. Why should he be able to fall in with everything strange right away?"

"We'll make it up when he comes back," said Mrs. Milford. "What did Mr. Truman say? Will you go down there for him today?"

"I told you. Truman was fuming. I hardly got any sense out of him, but I'm pretty sure Paul won't be coming back here in a hurry."

"Never?" wailed Etta. "I want him to come back."

"It doesn't really matter what we want," said her father. "We had our chance. I don't think we'll get another. We must be patient and see how things work out. Now they're saying something about Paul's father having turned up."

"Father!" exclaimed Mrs. Milford. "Fine father. He doesn't ever appear to have seen his own son. Surely that won't make any difference when we've said we're ready to adopt him?"

"It rather depends on whether Paul wants to be adopted," Mr. Milford said wearily. "We'd better let the whole thing rest, I think. There's nothing we can do now. We let Paul down pretty badly, and Mr. Truman and the rest of them are trying to sort it out. We'll just have to keep out of it for a while."

"But I want Paul to come back now," Etta said.

"Maybe what we all want is the idea of having someone," her father said. "It's easy enough to have good ideas. When it comes to people, it's a little harder to make things work."

Mr. Truman came back from his phoning session looking rumpled and exhausted. He was also much quieter. Mrs. Truman noticed this and nodded knowingly at Paul.

"It's no good," Mr. Truman said. "No one starts work at this time of the morning. I'm just wasting time calling offices with no one in them. I'll try again. Meanwhile we'd better get you settled, young man."

"Settled?" said Paul. "You mean I can stay here?"

"Well, of course. Where else? You'd better come with

me now and I'll tell the housemother you're back for now."

Paul didn't feel exactly happy going up the familiar path to the house, but at least it was somewhere he knew and where there wouldn't be any surprises. Also he was extremely tired, having walked at least ten of the twenty-five miles to Magsted during the night. A kindhearted bus driver had let him ride free the rest of the way.

Mr. Truman handed him over to the housemother with instructions that he was to be allowed to go to bed and sleep as long as he wanted to, then he patted Paul on the head and went back to his office.

He stood by his desk, tapping the wood with his fingers and thinking. Still too early to phone anyone. He went around to the filing cabinet and got Paul's file out. Then he opened it on the desk and sat down to study it.

The office door was thrown violently open, striking the wall with a bang. Mr. Truman jumped as if he had been shot and looked up. In the doorway stood a youngish man in a strange garment that covered his head like a monk's hood. He had a wide, determined mouth, a short-clipped beard, and old-fashioned steel-rimmed glasses.

Mr. Truman was in no mood for surprises. "Who the hell are you?" he demanded fiercely.

"My name is Aintree," said the man. "Hugh Aintree."

14 . My Sort of Person

"And about time, too," said Mr. Truman. "Come in and sit down."

Hugh Aintree didn't move immediately. He leaned the top half of his body forward a little and gave the office a thorough inspection, as if trying to judge whether it was safe for him to enter. He paid particular attention to the small woollen mat across the doorway, and finally decided to be on the safe side and step right over it. Then he unzipped the green monkish garment and dropped it in a heap in one corner of the room.

Mr. Truman, watching him closely all this time, now saw a powerfully built young man, short but with wide, strong shoulders and rather long arms. He was dressed in a red T shirt, jeans, and sandals. He sat down on the chair rather as a sparrow hawk rests for a moment on a fence post—ready to be away again in a moment.

"You're Truman," he said.

"That's right."

"I've come about Paul. I'd like to see him."

"After eight years? What's all the hurry?"

"I didn't say I was in a hurry," said Hugh Aintree. "And I last saw Paul six years ago, just before I left for the Antarctic. Why are you being so edgy with me? Have I done something to annoy you?"

Mr. Truman leaned back in his chair and slowly let his bunched-up shoulders relax. Then he laughed. "I am on edge," he admitted. "Sorry if I seemed to be taking it out on you. So you went to the Antarctic? Go on."

"I'm a meteorologist."

"Weatherman?"

"If you like. My wife and I separated, and I did a two-year tour with the Australian team down there."

"That was six years ago?"

"Then had two years knocking around on weather ships and such, then another two years on the ice. I got back to England a month ago."

Mr. Truman chuckled to himself. "I'd love to see Miss Mallim's face when I tell her this," he said.

"I've already told her," said Aintree. "She was very odd. She was all embarrassed and then started apologizing. Why do you think she did that?"

"It was your letter. You said something about being out of touch for some time and she jumped to the conclusion you'd been in prison or in a mental home or something."

"What a strange idea."

"Not really. Quite a lot of our parents are in one or the other. But that's neither here nor there. I'd better fill in the picture for you."

Mr. Truman explained all that had been going on. He told Aintree about the Milfords, about Paul's time in the Home, about the foster parents in Maidstone.

"The kid's had a rough time," Aintree commented.

"Most of the children here have had a rough time," said Mr. Truman. "It's not much fun for kids when a family splits up, you know."

"I thought she'd marry again," Aintree said. "She was only a girl. How was I to know she'd go and die like that?"

"Are you telling me you didn't know anything about it?"

"I found out two weeks ago. That's why I started trying to find out where Paul was. But you people take such a long time to answer inquiries . . . you don't think I'd have stayed on the other side of the world if I'd known my . . . my son . . . needed me."

Mr. Truman heaved a long sigh. "I never know what to expect of people," he said. "Some people leave their children on station platforms. Some people put their children into a home and then want them back when they're old enough to earn money. I've seen everything in this job. I'm not surprised anymore. Now what are your plans for Paul?"

"I think we ought to meet."

"That's a modest request. And then what?"

"How can I tell? Better leave it to Paul. If he approves of me, then that's all right."

"And if he doesn't?"

"I don't know. Keep in touch, I suppose, in case he changes his mind."

"Right. Then what are we waiting for?" said Mr. Truman, and he stood up.

"Can I get to see him now?"

"Of course. That's what you came for."

"Don't I have to sign any forms?"

Mr. Truman grinned. "I see you've had trouble with the department. We have to be careful, you know. Right, then. Are you coming?"

When they reached the house, the housemother said that Paul had gone to bed but that she didn't know if he was asleep yet.

"I'll go up and see," said Mr. Truman, and then to

Aintree, "Look, you stroll around on the grass out there where Paul can see you from the window."

Aintree laughed. "So's he can inspect the goods before making a purchase?" he said.

"Weren't you ever a child?" asked Mr. Truman irritably. "If you're out there on the lawn, he can look at you and get used to you without having to make a quick decision, can't he? As long as you're a decent way off, he still has room to maneuver. As soon as you push your hairy adult face up close to him, he'll feel rushed. He'll feel he's got to say yes or no right away."

"I guess you're right. After all, you're the expert."

"I'm no expert," said Truman. "I just bleed easily."

Hugh Aintree smiled and went off in the direction of the large lawn at the side of the house. Mr. Truman took the first flight of stairs two stairs at a time but then stopped and leaned his forehead on the cool of the banister.

"Are you all right, Mr. Truman?" asked the house-mother from below.

Mr. Truman laughed a little with embarrassment. "Quite all right, thanks. Just mumbling a little prayer."

He went on up more slowly and into the dormitory. Paul was lying in bed but with his hands behind his head and his eyes open wide.

"Not asleep then?"

"I don't really feel sleepy now. I had a huge bath. Up to my neck nearly."

"Well, if you're that wide awake, you'll be just in the mood for some good news I've got."

Mr. Truman sat on the end of the bed and began to tell Paul all about his surprise visitor. Paul didn't ask any questions; he just got more and more excited, his eyes opening wider and wider. "Where is he now?" he cried at the end of it all.

"Look out of that window and you should be able to catch a glimpse of him."

Paul leaped out of bed and ran to the window. "Where?" he demanded. "I can't see anyone!"

Mr. Truman followed more slowly. The lawn was empty. There was no sign of anyone anywhere. Then a branch of a tree on the edge of the lawn moved. It sagged down. The leaves shook furiously.

"There he is!" shouted Paul.

Hugh Aintree was hanging by his toes from a branch ten feet above the ground. He hung there for a few seconds like some large ripe fruit, then he dropped, doubled up in the air, and landed on his feet. He bowed seriously to the house and then turned smartly and began to pace up and down the lawn with his hands clasped behind his back.

"Show-off!" said Mr. Truman good-humouredly.

"Is that him?"

"Yes, that's him all right. Do you want to go down?"

"I don't know. You go and talk to him and I'll get dressed. Don't let him go away, though."

"He won't go away. He's not that sort."

Mr. Truman went downstairs and out onto the lawn. Hugh Aintree grinned boyishly at him. "How was that for a commercial?" he asked.

They walked up and down together talking for about ten minutes, but Paul did not make an appearance. Aintree kept looking toward the house.

"Give him time," said Mr. Truman. "He's got to catch up on six years."

Mr. Truman sat down on the grass. Hugh Aintree sat,

leaned on one elbow, then sprawled out flat like a stranded starfish. He half closed his eyes against the sun.

"While we've a moment," said Mr. Truman, "we'd better think about the legal side of all this. You realize you won't be allowed simply to walk off with Paul, even if he wants to go?"

"I guessed it wouldn't be that easy."

"How do you live?"

"At the moment in a trailer. I've booked up to do a lecture tour. I go to schools and show pictures of the Antarctic and give talks on what it's like down there. I'm booked up for the next year."

"You couldn't take Paul with you. What about school and so on? Anyway, you know what the law is. They wouldn't call that a proper 'establishment.' "

"I'll settle down by and by," Aintree said. "Could Paul stay with you until I've got this 'establishment'?"

"That would be one solution."

"Well, then . . ."

"Hi!" The shout came from the house. Both men looked up to see Paul, dressed, leaning out of his dormitory window.

"Are you really my father?"

Aintree jumped up and walked toward the house. "That's right."

"Were you really at the South Pole?"

"Yes."

"What was it like?"

"Very cold."

"Did you see any penguins?"

"Thousands."

Paul seemed to be considering his next question. Then

he said, "Have you been in prison?"

"No."

"In a mental home?"

"No."

"Are you sure?"

"Quite sure. Have you?"

Paul laughed. "Of course not." He began to climb out onto the window ledge. Mr. Truman opened his mouth to call but then closed it again and only muttered to himself. Aintree moved closer but stood relaxed with his hands on his hips.

"Is it too far to jump?" Paul asked.

Aintree felt the lawn with his heel. "Too hard," he said. "You'd go splat!"

"Can you catch me?"

Aintree judged the distance. Mr. Truman muttered to himself even more fiercely and then turned his back on them both.

"Turn around and hang by your hands," Aintree said.

"What's wrong with the stairs?" Mr. Truman said. He was speaking to himself, but they both heard him. They smiled at each other in a pitying way. Paul turned around and hung by his hands. Aintree stood underneath and reached up until he could hold Paul's feet.

"Now let go but keep leaning against the wall."

He lowered Paul's feet until they were on his shoulders, then he held his hands up again for Paul to hold. He turned and walked across the lawn with Paul standing up on his shoulders. "Hup!" he said and Paul jumped for the ground.

"Now what?" said Paul.

Aintree thought a moment. "I know. Come and see my Land Rover."

Father and son went off down the path; Mr. Truman was left standing alone on the lawn. He ruffled his hair ruefully and followed. He caught up with them again out on the road, where Aintree had left his Land Rover. It was painted a frightening yellow and the back was heaped with all sorts of gear.

"We're going for a run," Aintree said as soon as Mr. Truman came up. "That's all right, I suppose?"

"Er . . . yes . . . of course . . ."

Less than a minute later the yellow vehicle was out of sight around the first corner in a cloud of dust. Mrs. Truman came out of the house and saw her husband standing in the roadway.

"What was all that noise?"

"You've just missed the Aintrees, father and son."

"Did they take to each other?"

"Like a magnet and a two-inch nail. I hope something can be arranged for them. They deserve a break." He followed his wife into the house. "On the other hand," he said abruptly, "that Hugh Aintree seems like the sort of man who could make his own arrangements."

Around the middle of the afternoon the Aintrees returned. For a second time that day Mr. Truman's door crashed back against the wall and Mr. Truman looked up from his desk to see the two of them, glowing, on his doormat. "Have a good time?" he said.

"Splendid."

"No doubts? No . . . troubles?"

"Of course not," said Hugh Aintree. "Can't you see, Paul's my kind of person."

"Yes," said Mr. Truman. "It did strike me, as a matter of fact. What have you been up to?"

"Everything," said Paul. "We went for a swim, we had fish and chips, he showed me his trailer—you ought to see it—and he does paintings—real ones—with oil paint. He's done some of the South Pole and the Aurora Aus——"

"Australis," prompted Aintree.

"That's right. And icebergs, and you should see the colors. I thought it was all white there, but it's not."

"All sounds very exciting," said Mr. Truman.

"And we've also fixed up what we're going to do," added Hugh Aintree quietly.

"Oh, you have, have you?"

"Yes. You can get your official forms and things out later and make it all legal. But we've fixed it up."

"I had a feeling you might," said Truman.

"Well, we went to see the Milfords . . ."

"You did *what?*"

"Went to see the Milfords. Paul wanted to show me off, I think. We got on famously. They really are a nice family. And that girl . . . she's a wonder . . ."

"Are we talking about the same people?" asked Mr. Truman. "The way I heard it, Paul and Etta did nothing but quarrel."

"Quarrel? Man, they fought like cat and dog from the moment we got there. You should have heard it."

"That's good, is it?"

"Of course it is. They just like to fight. Didn't you know that?"

"I think I must have been living on another planet," said Mr. Truman. "Or perhaps I'm just getting old."

"Do you want to hear what we fixed?"

"Please go on."

"Paul wants to go back there. The Milfords will foster him, or whatever you call it, and while I'm doing this lecture bit I'll get back there weekends and holidays. Mrs. Milford says I can put my camp bed up in Paul's bedroom and stay with them. At the end of the year we take stock and see how things are going. How's that?"

"I don't believe it," said Mr. Truman.

Hugh Aintree picked up the phone and handed it to Mr. Truman. "Care to call them up and check?"

"I most certainly will."

He dialed the number and waited. After a while a voice

answered. "This is Truman here. From the Magsted Children's Home. Mr. Aintree has just been telling me . . . yes . . . yes, he's right here beside me. . . ." He put his hand over the phone and said to Paul, "It's Etta. She seems to be pretty annoyed about something."

"Well, ask her what's the matter," said Paul, grinning.

The voice on the phone squeaked away for a long time like an infuriated mouse. Mr. Truman held the phone at some distance from his ear. When the voice stopped for a moment he said to Paul, "She seems to be accusing you of letting her rabbit out of its hutch. She says she's searched everywhere and can't find it and if you don't tell her where it is she'll never talk to you again."

"Tell her . . ." began Paul.

"No, you tell her," said Mr. Truman firmly and handed him the phone.

"Wild animals shouldn't be kept in cages," said Paul into the phone. The furious mouse at the other end seemed to go completely off its head at this.

"I thought it would like a nice comfortable bed," said Paul.

"Whose bed?" said the mouse.

"Yours, of course," said Paul and quickly handed the phone back to Mr. Truman.

"Etta, listen . . . yes, I know. He's a dreadful child. You'll have to train him into more civilized ways . . . yes . . . well now, before you go searching for your rabbit, will you get your father or mother to the phone . . . yes, I'll hang on. . . ."

Hugh Aintree looked at his son. "Shall we leave him to it?" he said. "Let's go and climb a few trees."

"All right," said Paul.

8